Elaine Goodale Eastman, Dora Read Goodale

Apple-blossoms; verses of two children

Elaine Goodale Eastman, Dora Read Goodale

Apple-blossoms; verses of two children

ISBN/EAN: 9783337215477

Printed in Europe, USA, Canada, Australia, Japan

Cover: Foto ©Andreas Hilbeck / pixelio.de

More available books at **www.hansebooks.com**

APPLE-BLOSSOMS

VERSES OF TWO CHILDREN

ELAINE GOODALE
DORA READ GOODALE

NEW YORK
G. P. PUTNAM'S SONS
182 FIFTH AVENUE
1878

PREFACE.

Child-life, self-expressed, is something so rare in
literature that a few explanatory words seem fit in
offering this little volume to the public.

These verses are, above all else, fresh and spon-
taneous, the almost unconscious outflow of two
simple, wholesome lives, in their earliest youth. By
their grace and purity they have given perennial
delight to the family circle, that favorable audience
for which alone they were written.

Yet they are but apple-blossoms, the delicate
garlands with which New England orchards wake
in loveliness. If now, willing to share them with
other kindly hearts that love true and simple things,
we find that we have offered too slight a bouquet in
the market-places, we shall await with patience the
fruitage of the coming years.

The future, with its serious responsibilities and earnest labor, its faithful devotion to the service of God's Truth and Beauty, must bring the ripe work which searching criticism shall test, and Time himself shall weigh.

D. H. R. G.

SKY FARM, *August 1, 1878.*

Dedication

TO OUR MOTHER.

THE LOWLIEST BLOSSOM OF THE SPRING,
    BY RAIN AND SUNLIGHT FED,
TO LIMPID BLUE AND PEARLY CLOUD
    UPLIFTS ITS DROOPING HEAD.

EVEN SO, WITH IMPULSE WARM, WE BRING
    THE BLOOM OF INFANCY,
THE FRAGRANCE OF OUR EARLIEST YEARS,
    O MOTHER DEAR, TO THEE!

THE LOVE THAT GAVE US LIFE AND STRENGTH,
    THAT GUARDED DAY BY DAY,
WHAT TENDEREST WORDS CAN HALF EXPRESS?
    WHAT ANSWERING LOVE REPAY?

YET TAKE THE FRESH AND SIMPLE WREATH
    WHOSE EVERY FLOWER IS THINE,
TILL RIPER YEARS THEIR TRIUMPHS BRING,
    TO OFFER AT THY SHRINE.

CONTENTS.

POEMS BY ELAINE GOODALE.

POEMS BY DORA READ GOODALE.

POEMS.

ELAINE GOODALE.

Born, *Oct. 9th*, 1863.

APPLE-BLOSSOMS.

APPLE-BLOSSOM TIME.

THE sky is rich in shimmering sheen
　　Of deep, delicious blue ;
The earth is freshly, softly green,
　　Of one translucent hue ;
The choir of birds in wood and field
　　Ring out a happy chime ;
The trees their fairest foliage yield
　　In apple-blossom time.

The orchard rows are all ablush,
　　The meadows all aglow ;
On every bough a vivid flush,
　　A drift of petalled snow ;
The clustered bloom, with faint perfume,
　　Wreathes many a garland fine,
And many a rosy, nodding plume
　　In apple-blossom time.

The fullness of our early dreams,
　Tho' fresh and pure and sweet
When the glad earth with beauty teems,
　Soon trembles to our feet ;
Richer, tho' rarer, comes the fruit
　To crown a golden prime,
Fulfilling pledges proffered us
　In apple-blossom time.

THE LAST HAREBELL.

PLUCK the harebell, fading fast,
    Little one !
Pluck it, for it blooms the last—
    Summer's done.

For the harebell comes in June,
    Bright and blue,
Lasts until October's noon—
    Blooms for you.

So love, darling, for my sake,
    Sweet harebell,
Drooping fair on stony brake,
    Hill or dell.

Graceful harebell, lovely flower !
    Tho' we part,
Come again in Summer's hour—
    Cheer my heart !

AUTUMN.

NATURE hath cast her summer robes,
    Her bonny robes of green,
She wears her Autumn colors now,
    In brighter tints she's seen.

A wreath of gentians crowns her brow,
    And harebells kiss her feet ;
The soft breeze wafts o'er woods and fields
    A fragrance passing sweet.

The purple asters bloom in crowds
    In every shady nook,
And ladies' eardrops deck the banks
    Of many a babbling brook.

O Autumn, stay ! your flowers renew,
    And brighter paint your leaves,
'Twould break our hearts to have you go
    With fruits and golden sheaves !

AN APPEAL TO MAY.

COME forth and cheer us, dainty May !
  Come forth ! thou canst no more delay ;
Thy tender buds, in haste to blow,
Are checked and chilled by frost and snow ;
We sigh for thee, both night and day,
Then come and cheer us, gentle May !

The poets shout thee to the skies ;
But lo ! their murmur fainting dies,
'Tis frozen in the cloudy grey,—
Now colder greetings welcome May ;
Then melt it, Love, and make it thine,
  And all shall hail thee, May divine !

SORROW.

WEARILY sigheth Sorrow's wind
   Over meadow and moor,
Wearily sigheth Sorrow's wind
   Over the rich and poor,
Till it cometh to a cottage door,
Where it hath never been before.

Sadly it moaneth at the door,
   But they will not let it in ;
Outside Sorrow and Sin may roar,
   Sweet Sunshine reigns within ;
Sin cannot conquer, nor Sorrow slay,
Where a smiling spirit dwells alway.

Then Death spreads out his great black wings,
   And covers up their day ;
But the angel fair that guards the house,
   Wipes all their tears away ;
It whispers softly, " God knows best,"
And to His grace they leave the rest.

SONG FOR THE LAST NIGHT OF THE

OLD YEAR.

REST, weary ones, serenely rest
    Upon the Old Year's gentle breast !
Ere yet again you wake from sleep,
His faithful heart will cease to beat ;
    No more, no more, alas ! no more
    You'll sleep in 1874.

Weep, fill your eyes with tender tears,
Weep for the old forgotten years,
Weep for the year about to die,
Softly and sadly say good-bye ;
    No more, no more, alas ! no more
    You'll weep in 1874.

Kiss, wrathful ones, forgive and kiss ;
Do not the Old Year thus dismiss,
Let not the happy New Year in
To bosoms filled with grief or sin ;
    Forgive and kiss, nor linger more
    While yet 'tis 1874.

Smile, troubled ones, be glad and smile,
O let your joy be free from guile !
Smile to the sad, a cheerful beam
May help them on thro' life's dark stream :
    Weep for the Old Year yet alive,
    But smile on 1875 !

THE FALLING SNOW.

THE snow it falleth so soft and slow,
  This beautiful, busy night ;
The mists reach down to the earth below,
  And all is one sheet of white.

The snow it falleth so soft and slow,
  From the angels' clouded bars ;
The feathery flakes at the window blow
  And dot it with tiny stars:

The snow it falleth so soft and slow,
  O'er the grave of the dying day ;
Earth's rounded bosom is full of woe,
  And the skies wear a shroud of grey.

The snow it falleth so soft and slow,
  Thro' the veil of the darkening night ;
Till the morning dawns in a rosy glow,
  And the sky is blue and bright.

NIGHT AND MORNING.

ONE is clad in snowy garments,
　　Purer, fairer than the lily,
And her cheeks are like to rosebuds,
Dewy, dainty, morning rosebuds,
Opening first to air and sunshine,
First revealing all their beauty,
All their hidden, maiden beauty,
First from soft, green wraps unfolding
All their tender, rosy blushes—
And her locks are soft and golden,
Scattering a light around her
Nothing else can shed or scatter,
Wooing all the lights of day dawn,
Lovelier than all or any ;
And her eyes are bluer, brighter,
Softer, deeper, clearer, fairer
Than the azure of the heavens
In the month that Earth doth boast of,—
June—and may she live forever !

And forever live the Princess,
Morning, sweet, celestial Morning,
Whose bright eyes do bear her colors !

But the other creepeth softly,
Draped in her own flowing tresses,
Dark as only Night can make them,
Lighted up with eyes as starry
As the brightest orb in Heaven ;
Shaded by her silken lashes
As the stars by clouds are shaded ;—
Cheeks as rosy red as coral,
Ocean-kissed, fresh budding coral,—
Rose-flushed limbs lapt in the twilight
Of the golden summer evening.

SPRING SONG.

O THE little streams are running,
      Running, running !—
O the little streams are running
      O'er the lea ;
And the green, soft grass is springing,
      Springing, springing !—
And the green, soft grass is springing,
      Fair to see.

In the woods the breezes whisper,
      Whisper, whisper !—
In the woods the breezes whisper
      To the flowers ;
And the robins sing their welcome,
      Welcome, welcome !—
And the robins sing their welcome—
      Happy hours !

Over all the sun is shining,
      Shining, shining !—
Over all the sun is shining
      Clear and bright,
Flooding bare and waiting meadows,
      Meadows, meadows !—
Flooding bare and waiting meadows
      With his light.

THE COMING OF THE BIRDS.

ON St. Valentine's Day,
    As the legends say,
Each birdling chooses a mate,—
    Here, mantled in snow,
    Rude Winter says "No,"
And hopefully still we must wait.

    But when violets peep
    From the hillside steep,
And over them hums the bee,
    Then merrily home
    The wild birds come,—
A bright little band to see.

    Familiar and fair,
    Their wings cleave the air,
And quiver, and flutter, and dally,
    And each liquid note
    From a fresh-tuned throat,
Rings clear over woodland and valley.

O follow ! O follow !
Thou lingering swallow,—
The robin and blue bird are here ;
   'Mid the tender leaves,
   'Neath the dusky eaves,
Come, twitter and chirp your cheer !

   Over dewy red clover,
   Each gay little rover
May circle, and chatter, and play ;
   For a day he may wait,
   With his gentle brown mate,
Till the home-life calls him away.

   Then he'll build him a house
   'Mid the tangled boughs ;
And in sunny summer weather,
   In the quiet wood
   He will rear a brood,
He and his love together.

SPRING RAIN.

THE wind brushes briskly and busily by,
    O'er the gracious expanse of the tender
    blue sky,
And the misty white veils that about her will crowd,
Are silently gathered in pillars of cloud.

The warm vapor skyward no longer can stay,
It melts into rain and it patters away ;
Each drop, as below in the earth it doth creep,
Awakens a flower from its long winter's sleep.

The grass, dead and brown, at its touch groweth
    green,
The bud yet unopened, a blossom is seen ;
All nature is started to vigor again
At the magical call of the soft-falling rain.

TRAILING ARBUTUS.

DEEP in the lonely forest,
  High on the mountain side,
Long is the dreary winter,
  Short is the summer tide ;
Just in the breath between them,
  Pregnant with sun and showers,
Starts from the earth primeval
  Fairest of northern flowers.

All through the sunny summer,
  Lavish with wealth of bloom,
She, too, hath shared life's fullness,
  Hid in her forest gloom ;
Nurtured with dews and sunlight,
  Richly her buds are fed,
Fresh, while the summer fadeth,
  Fresh, when its flowers are dead.

Then when the rude winds seek her,
  Threaten her buds to blast,
Fiercely assailed by Winter,
  Fearless she holds them fast,

Fast, till the spring draws nearer;
   Fast till the days grow fair;
Fast, till the April showers
   Quicken the chilly air.

Waked by the murmuring breezes,
   Kissed by the shining sun,
Up in a burst of transport
   Starteth the prisoned one ;—
Blushing in airy clusters,
   Pressing a mossy bed,
Leaves of autumnal russet
   Over her soft couch shed.

Close to the damp earth clinging,
   Tender, and pink, and shy ;
Lifting her waxen blossoms
   . Up to the changeful sky :—
Welcome ! our springtide darling,
   Fresh in thy virgin hue;
Long as the oaks stand round thee,
   Yearly thy charms renew !

SPRING.

HARK ! the breezes tremble
    With the sighs of April ;—
See her sweeping northward,
    Spring ! our Spring !
Lingering, still we love her,
Still we smile and beckon,
As we hear the rustling
    Of her wing.

Nearer, nearer, nearer !
Dearer, dearer, dearer !
Flying ever onward
    Comes the Spring.
What tho' cloud-veils sometime
Dim her eyes of azure ?
Ah, the rarest pleasure
    Tears may bring !

Flowers mark her pathway,—
Violets' dewy blueness,

Blooming sweet and lowly,
       Heralds Spring ;
Dear arbutus, fairest,
Rosiest and rarest,
In the shaded woodlands
       Doth she fling.

Green the grass is growing,
Babbling brooks are flowing,
Birds their clearest, chanting
       For the Spring :
Ah, we too forgive her !
Ah, we too embrace her !
In our thrill of transport
       We, too, sing !

———

O wild azalea, rosy red,
   In every woody hollow ;
Put out, put out your pretty head,
   That I may see and follow !
That I may see and follow, dear,
   That I may see and follow !

THE QUEEN OF MAY.

WHERE the quivering sunbeam glances
  Thro' green dells and mossy glades,
Where the breeze so gaily dances
 In among the cooling shades,
Happy children laugh and play,
Clustered round their Queen of May.

On the young grass fresh and tender,
 Violets blooming at her feet,
Tiny form so still and slender,
 Tiny face so fair and sweet ;
Pure and plain her snowy dress,
Rare her childlike loveliness.

Drooping wreaths of rosy blossom
 Touch the cheek more pink than they,
Dimpled arms and creamy bosom
 Hath the maiden Queen of May ;
In her hand, for sceptre, holding
Branch of buds scarce yet unfolding.

Sea-blue eyes of wondrous clearness,
   Clustering ringlets, chestnut brown ;--
Three years old ! how bright and fearless !
   Well she merits such a crown ;
Pleased, yet shy, she smiles to me,—
Quaint her baby dignity.

In love only would she school us,
   Worthy of a May-tide reign ;
With a flowery rod she'd rule us,
   Bind us with a flowery chain ;
Still, so strong her sweet spells be,
From her feet we cannot flee.

Yet, my Queen, none reign forever,
   Quickly speed our sunniest hours ;
Would no weight might press thy forehead
   Heavier than thy wreath of flowers !
Taste thy joys, while yet they stay,
O belovéd Queen of May !

CONTRADICTIONS.

SKIES all of grey and blue,
   Skies all of clouds and rifts,
   Where gleaming sunlight shifts
      Tremblingly thro'.

Skies tender daffodil ;
   Dark mists bright tips disclose,
   Clear silver, amber, rose,—
      Drink, eyes, your fill !

Dense vapors o'er us rolled,
   Quick raindrops patter down,
   Sprinkling a starry crown—
      Showers of gold !

Brightest, and best, and last,
   The rainbow's arch is seen
   O'er meadows freshly green,—
      Our sunset's past.

JUNE COMES IN TO-MORROW.

COMPANIONS sweet,
Why do you weep,
And where is cause for sorrow?
"Alas, the May
Goes out to-day :—"
But June comes in to-morrow!

The glorious June!
With love and tune
It must not bring us sorrow;
Weep not, tho' May
Goes out to-day,
For June comes in to-morrow!

Why should we mourn
When life is gone,
This life so mixed with sorrow?
What tho' our May
Goes out to-day,—
Our June comes in to-morrow!

JUNE.

UNE ! June ! jubilant June !
    How shall I sing thee, or what can I say !
All, all, list to thy call,
Lost in the spell of a soft summer's day.
Come up, come up from the meadows sweet,
And our quickened pulses throb and beat ;—
Come down, come down from the woodlands green,
And we hail thee as our queen !
    Enchanting in beauty, bewitching in grace,
In freshness and tenderness pure and complete,
    Enraptured, we rest in thy loving embrace,
We joyously greet thee, we kneel at thy feet :—
        Beauteous bloom of all the year,
        June is here !

For stately trees in rich array ;
For sunlight all the happy day ;
    For blossoms radiant and rare ;
        For skies, when daylight closes ;
For joyous, clear, out-pouring song,
From birds that all the greenwood throng ;

For all things young, and bright, and fair ;
   We praise thee, month of roses !

For blue, blue skies of summer calm ;
For fragrant odors, breathing balm ;
   For quiet, cooling shades where oft
   The weary head reposes ;
For brooklets babbling thro' the fields,
Where Earth her choicest treasures yields ;
   For all things tender, sweet and soft ;
   We love thee, month of roses !

Smile, smile, on Britain's isle !
   Smile, smile, on Europe's main !
But here, but here, we hold thee dear,
   Smile on us once again !
For Berkshire Hills full well do know
The winter's cold and winter's snow,
And with thy smile, a happier throng
Shall swell the glad, exultant song :—
   Beauteous bloom of all the year,
   June is here !

A SONG TO SUMMER.

SUMMER ! thy heart is all too glad,
  Thy thoughts are all too bold,
Thou art too eager, thy hopes are mad,—
  My heart is calm and cold.

Hush that rich music from ripe red lips !
  Those burning glances are lost on me,—
They will not melt this heart of ice—
  They cannot melt it and set me free.

Thou canst not move me to smiles or tears—
  How foolish and fond thou art !
Thou canst not ravish these deaf, cold ears,
  Thou canst not thrill this heart.

Thy wreath of roses is heavy to wear,
  It will not rest on this calm, cold brow,—
A circlet of ice would better suffice—
  I would it were clasped there now !

I find insipid thy changeless sweet,
  And long for the respite that pain will give ;

Thy restless breezes, thy fever heat,
  Know not the shadow where I would live.

I love not the color that mantles thy cheek,
  I love not the fragrance and warmth of thy breath ;
The face I would see should no vain beauty seek,
  As pale as a snow drift, as haggard as Death.

Go, go ! cruel Summer ! hide, hide that fair face !
  Leave thy parching domain and thy withering
    throne !
Come, Winter ! I wait for thine icy embrace,—
  The chill of thy bosom responds to mine own.

ASHES OF ROSES.

SOFT on the sunset sky
    Bright daylight closes,
Leaving, when light doth die,
Pale hues that mingling lie,—
    Ashes of roses.

When Love's warm sun is set,
    Love's brightness closes ;
Eyes with hot tears are wet,
In hearts there linger yet
    Ashes of roses.

THE HARVEST MOON.

ON the waving fields of the ripened grain,
    That ripple and roll o'er the fertile plain ;
On their broad full sweep, and their ample room,
Shines the rich, round globe of the harvest moon.

On the golden sheaves of garnered wheat,
On the bearded rye, in stacks complete,
On the fresh buckwheat with its pink-white bloom,
Smiles the fair round face of the harvest moon.

On the busy reapers, with hearts so light,
Binding the sheaves thro' the early night,
Merrily humming a merry tune ;
Looks the well-pleased face of the harvest moon.

On the anxious owner, with busy care,
Proudly surveying the richness there ;
Driving away all thought of gloom,
Beams the kindly smile of the harvest moon.

THE ASTER.

BOLD are its footsteps in loneliest places,
  Scaling the steep crag and climbing
      height ;
Blossoming over with fairest young faces,
  Up the woodlands and far out of sight.

Light is its tread on the broad gracious meadow,
  Fringing the hedge-rows with purple and gold ;
Clustering softly in stillness and shadow,
  Freely and freshly its fringes unfold.

Close by the brookside 'tis twining and bending,
  Tenderly o'er the fair waters to lean ;
With the fresh current its life-blood is blending,—
  Pale, scattered petals drift down the cold stream.

Blossom on blossom crowds fairer and faster,
  Rich and yet simple its tint and array ;—
Drink we a health to the wild mountain aster,
  Star of ·the forest, the bank and the brae !

DEAD LEAVES.

HE forests that with Springtime were bursting
    into light,
  And spread to full, free Summer their canopies
    of green,
Fall, Nature's artist, painted with colors rich and
  bright,
  And all the Autumn landscape in warmest hues
    was seen.

They burned in gold and crimson, they burned
  themselves away,
  It left them brown and shrivelled, their panoply
    of flame ;
They danced upon the rattling boughs, they car-
  peted the way,
  They flung themselves upon the breeze without a
    home or name.

We call them dead : they rustle down and lie beneath our feet,
  They cover all the frosty ground, they fill the
    chilly air,

And tho' our tread above them seem softer and
    more sweet,
  The trees that once have loved them stand
    desolate and bare.

We call them dead : the dying year, perchance, may
    think them so,
  But a newer year will find them with newer
    beauties rife,—
When the sweet arbutus opens, and the early violets
    blow,
  They draw from last year's leafy mould their sus-
    tenance and life.

THE FAREWELL OF THE SEASONS.

WINTER.

A STILL, chill eve, 'twas Winter's last—
　　My brow throbbed hot and high ;
The silent hours were ebbing fast,
As thro' the door I lightly passed
　　Beneath the gloomy sky.

I gazed upon the frosted lawn,—
　　When lo ! in blank dismay
I saw a surging, ghostly throng,—
With muffled step they moved along ;
　　Silent and strange were they.

And at their head they still bore on,
　　Bore on, with faithful pride,
An old, old man in long, white gown—
His keen, blue eyes pierced to my own ;—
　　" Lo, Winter comes ! " they cried.

The snow lay deep ; the moon so pale
　　Shed faint her ghastly light ;

Hushed into awe was every gale ;—
He rose—I heard his mournful tale
   Ring on the listening night.

He said—" There is a fatal call,
   That fatal call hear I,
Yea, all must hear it, one and all ;
Each in his time must fade and fall,
   Must pine, and droop, and die.

" I hear the footsteps of the Spring,
   I feel her fragrant breath :
New hopes, new pleasures she will bring,
New songs her happy birds will sing,
   When I am cold in death.

" If you have loved me, love me still,
   If you have hated, hate,—
I never sought to do you ill,
Only my mission to fulfill,—
   Now, called, I cannot wait."

The clock struck twelve—he waved his hand,
   I heard him speak no more ;—
Gone ! he is gone ! A merry band
Ye shout the new friend o'er the land ;
   I weep the friend of yore.

SPRING.

The air was fresh, and warm the night,
 The grass and leaves were green,
The moon shed forth her clear, soft light ;
So ever pure, and calm, and bright,
 Spring's last, divinest scene.

When sudden on the stillness broke
 The sound of fairy horn ;
From cliff to cliff the echoes woke,
Then faint, more faint, in whispers spoke,
 And died as they were born.

I felt a quiver in the air,
 A step scarce brushed the grass ;
A stately form, so tall and fair,
A lovely face, beyond compare :—
 Spring ! Spring ! I saw her pass !

Clad dryad-like, a belt of gold
 Her gown of green confined,
A wreath of flowers and ferns enrolled
Drooped o'er her brow of dainty mould;
 Her brown locks flowed behind.

In her clear eyes of sky-born blue
 A tender gladness shone,

Tear-dropt, like violets wet with dew ;
Yet sad, and sweet, and strange, and true,
    Came forth her farewell tone.

" Past, past," she said, " are Springtide's hours,
    Pale dawn of Summer days !
I rear the buds with sun and showers,
And Summer turns them into flowers—
    To which belongs the praise ?

" From regions of eternal Spring,
    Love-armed, I sally forth ;
Youth, hope and loveliness I bring,
With birds that happy carols sing,
    To cheer the snow-bound North.

" Your weary, dreary, frozen land
    I tear from Winter's grasp ;
His cruel winds and storms withstand,
Till, drawn from out his icy hand,
    You feel my gentler clasp.

" And yet you taunt, and call me slow,
    And mock my patient care,
As if from Winter's frost and snow
At once the trees their leaves could show,
    And flowers bloom everywhere.

"Still, Earth I love, and tend, and own,
    I make it fair and sweet ;
Then lay my finished work adown,
To shine in Summer's glorious crown,
    And blossom 'neath her feet.

"When, with glad song and lightsome tread,
    Your hearts to June ye bring ;
Her throne above my fallen head,—
Forget not then what I have said,
    The farewell voice of Spring."

She spread her wings and upward flew ;
    Her form grew faint and far :
'Twas midnight—from the deepening blue
A midnight token proved her true—
    A single falling star.

SUMMER.

The sun had shone the livelong day
    Thro' cloud-veils misty white,
And now the fair moon's fainter ray
Like snow upon the meadows lay ;
    Subdued and pale her light.

The wayward breezes whispered low,
    And sighed in anxious pain ;

The roses lost their joyous glow,
All Nature breathed, above, below,—
  "Sweet Summer, come again ! "

Forth from the dusky robe of Night
    There broke a dazzling gleam,—
A sunny head, so fair, so bright,
All crowned with waves of quivering light,
    And garlanded with green !

Her large, soft eye of liquid hue,
    Tho' ofttimes clear and glad
With youth's delights, its sorrows knew ;
And now, tho' kind and tender too,
    Its every look was sad.

A rosebud mouth, a blooming cheek,
    A brow so pure and low,—
With eager eyes her charms I seek,
And long to hear those red lips speak,
    And Summer's song to know.

I look, I listen and—I hear !
    That clear and gracious voice,
Those words from one I hold so dear,
They draw the smile, the sigh, the tear ;
    They sadden and rejoice.

"Farewell!" she said, "my friends I greet;
How little time it seems
Since ye were falling at my feet,
And I was crowned with roses sweet,
And lapt in blissful dreams.

"Ah! well for me the rising tear
May dim those joyous eyes!
The happy climax of the year,
All Nature holds most rich and dear,
With me regretted dies.

"And if I merit aught of praise
Your love on me bestows,
One only last request I raise :—
Remember me thro' Autumn days,
Thro' Winter's cruel snows.

"Another year I come again,
To rule you as before :—"
One last farewell, one dying strain
Breathed softly o'er the silent plain—
And she was seen no more.

AUTUMN.

With lashing wind and sleety rain
The dreary midnight fell,—

A strange excitement filled my brain,
I could but wish to hear again
   A Season's last farewell.

So out upon the porch I stept
   From parlors light and warm :—
A fleeting Figure by me swept,
A wondrous Presence near me kept,
   Dim outlined thro' the storm.

The passion of his mournful cry
   I would you might have heard ;
O that rich voice, so deep and high,
That seemed to rend the very sky,
   Gave power to every word !

"O man ! man ! man ! whose petty cares
   Your selfish brains so fill,
The music of the mighty spheres,
The magic of the fleeting years,
   Leave ne'er a thought or thrill !

"I speak not for myself alone,
   That you may love me more,—
I would that you should learn to own,
And to revere the mighty throne,
   Where reign the Seasons four.

" I want a heart's responsive glow
    To every new delight ;
As changing seasons onward go,
In sweet accordance may they flow,
    In peace with man unite.

" While Springtime conquered Winter wild,
    Preparing Summer's way,
I weaned your hearts from Summer mild,
And yet to Winter reconciled,
    With tenderest delay.

" I would you should extend your cares
    Beyond mere petty gains ;
The music of the heavenly spheres,
The magic of the varying years,
    Be more than empty names.

" And lastly, may you find a tongue
    In every flake or flower,
Remembering long the meaning wrung
From accents of an unknown tongue,
    That speaks to you this hour."

A sudden gust flew whistling by,
    I caught an eager breath—
Mixed with gray clouds that dimmed the sky,
I saw a misty Figure lie,
    Tossed in a stormy death.

"TOUCH US GENTLY, GENTLY, TIME."

IN the spring of early years,
   With its budding hopes and fears;
  In the summer's glowing prime;
In the autumn's lonely grief,
Fading light and falling leaf;
   Touch us gently, gently, Time.

On the bud of promise sweet
Lavish no too fervent heat,—
   Clearly, purely, softly shine;
Let not childhood lose too soon
All its fresh, unconscious bloom;
   Touch us gently, gently, Time.

Let no maddening bliss or pain,
Let no hot impatience stain
   A serenely golden prime:
Soothe with cool, soft fingers now
Throbbing heart and burning brow;
   Touch us gently, gently, Time.

Let no dark forebodings fill,
Startle by no sudden chill
  Of a harsh, capricious clime ;
Lead us by thy quiet ways,
Frosty nights, and mellow days ;
  Touch us gently, gently, Time.

When our harvest's reaped at last,
Hopes fulfilled, and labors past,
  Softly bright our years' decline ;
Let our spent life glide away
Like an Indian Summer's day ;
  Touch us gently, gently, Time.

Twilight shadows o'er us creep—
We are weary ; let us sleep :
  Farewell Earth, and all that's thine !
Now, while here our eyelids close
In a last, a long repose,
  Close them gently, gently, Time.

CHRISTMAS EVE.

IS Christmas Eve. The twilight creepeth stilly,
  To hush with restful calm the busy day ;
O'er snow-lapt fields the darkness gathers chilly,
  And slowly fades the sunset's paling ray.

Hushed is the household's varying commotion,
  And silently about the fire we sit ;
Loosed is the tension of a strained emotion,
  The chord of life with which our hearts are knit.

The flickering firelight, and the shadows falling,
  We follow with unconscious, dreamy gaze,
The living present lost in dim recalling
  The joys or sorrows of our bygone days.

'Tis Christmas Eve ! A sacred peace is stealing
  Upon the aching heart, and weary brain,
An undefined, a sweet and holy feeling
  Stills the quick throbbing of a restless pain.—

We lost Thee in the hour of dark temptation,
  Forgot to look for succor from above,—
We find Thee, O our heart's Divine Salvation !
  Bring Thy sweet messages of peace and love !

LIFE IN DEATH.

GOLDEN-GLEAMING, silver-shining,
　　Soft with amethyst's purple light,
Tenderly the twilight shadows
　　Deepen into night.

Flaming crimson, amber yellow,
　　Brighten round us far and near ;
Autumn with her richest glories
　　Lights the dying year.

Why should'st thou, O man immortal !
　　Dim thy sunset's farewell ray,
Darken Death's mysterious portal—
　　Gate to endless day !

TRANSFIGURED.

SILENTLY away, away,
  Glides the day,
   Underneath her misty robes,
All of grey.

Close her dark mists settle down,
O'er the crown
   Of the mountains, tipped with clear
Golden brown.

Ah, what ray so glad and bright
Cheers my sight?
   Parting, breaking, see the clouds
Fringed with light!

Soft and clear the sunset air!
Fresh and fair
   Dreamy hues that blush and mingle,
New and rare!

Robed in purple, glides the day
Still away,
   At her feet red roses tremble
In the grey.

A BROOK LIFE.

FAR, far up on the distant mountain,
  Deep in a forest wild and lone,
Bubbling out in the shaded stillness,
  Welling up by a mossy stone ;
Overflowing its cool, green basin,
  Trickling out in a tiny rill,
Creeping under the tangled brushwood,
  Threading its way adown the hill ;

Widening out into sunny shallows,
  Gurgling down in some hidden deep,
Foaming over the rocky ledges,
  Murmuring on thro' the fields asleep ;
Filling the cups of the lowly flowers,
  Bathing the feet of the stately trees,
Winding and leaping, twisting and turning,
  Babbling of blossoms, and birds, and bees ;

Hurrying down the rugged mountain,
  Dipping into the gentle dale,
Growing quieter, calmer, deeper,
  Over the slopes of the peaceful vale ;

Yet with a dash of its wide, wild freedom,
    Yet with a freshness all its own,
Under its mellow, musical murmur
    Ringing out in a clearer tone ;

Flowing on thro' the fair, bright morning,
    Flowing still thro' the noonday heat,
Cooling the parched lips, gently laving
    Aching forehead and fevered cheek ;
Bringing a draught of pure, sweet water
    Down to the dry and dusty plain ;
Bringing a breath of life and freshness,
    Cheering anew the languid brain :

Slowly growing a mighty river,
    Broad, and gracious, and deep, and grand,
Gladdening every thirsty valley,
    Watering all the barren land ;
Gathering in to its rolling volume
    Baby streamlets from hill and dale,
Bearing up on its swelling bosom
    Bounding bark and shifting sail :

Yet with its great force pressing onward
    Over the country, far and wide,
Freighted with human lives and fortunes,
    Reaching at last the ocean side ;

Giving at last its whole existence,
   Fresh, and constant, and pure, and free,
Into the blue gulf yet unfathomed,
   Into the depths of the boundless sea.

THE FIRST FLOWERS.

WHEN our eyes are weary, weary
    Of the brown and barren fields,
When we yearn with tender longing
    For the bloom that summer yields,
O what new and sudden rapture
    Makes our languid pulses start,
As we find the first spring flowers,
    Dearest to the hungry heart !

Then the banks are golden-studded,
    Where the brown brook babbles by,
And the wooded slope beyond it
    Gives a dream of April sky,
In the blossoms closely crowded,
    Purple, blue, and cloudy white,
Clustered deep in silent shadow,
    Touched with bloom of softened light.

Then the starry, fragile wind-flower,
    Poised above in airy grace,
Virgin white, suffused with blushes,
    Shyly droops her lovely face ;

And far up the rugged hillside,
    Spring and Hope in every breath,
Pure and perfect, sweet arbutus
    Twines her rosy-tinted wreath.

Flowers of spring, O first and fairest !
    Welcome to our snow-bound earth !
No rich bloom or stately splendor
    Can eclipse your humble birth ;
'Tis a new and sudden rapture
    Makes our languid pulses start,
When we find the first spring flowers,
    Dearest to the hungry heart.

PAPA'S BIRTHDAY.

 DEAR Sky Farm ! O rare Sky Farm !
  Rejoice, to-day, rejoice !
Unite your many tongues to ours
  In one harmonious voice ;
Ye winsome warblers of the wood,
  Pour forth your clarion lays,
And welcome to the happy earth
  This happiest of days !

For 'tis the anniversary
  Of his auspicious birth,
Who singled out from all the world
  This cherished spot of earth ;
Who brought a loved and loving wife
  To grace its haunts so wild,
And, with its blessing, thrice became
  The father of a child.

It is his birthday who has tilled
  Its acres broad and fair,
Has reaped its golden harvest fields,
  And breathed its balmy air ;

Whose holy, happy home it is,
  With mother, children, wife,
Whose vine-clad cottage crowns the hill,
  Brimful of health and life.

O dear Sky Farm! O rare Sky Farm!
  Break out in brighter bloom,
And waft o'er all the emerald fields
  Your incense of perfume!
Deep heavens of celestial blue,
  Watch o'er him, guard and bless
Thro' many a sun-lit birthday more
  Of love and happiness!

May warmer union bind our hearts
  Together from this hour,
And draw us closer to our farm
  With deep and sacred power!
Grant every highest, purest joy,
  Protect from every harm,
The planter of our precious home,
  The founder of Sky Farm!

MY WINDOW CURTAIN.

LET others round their windows
    Loop folds of flimsy lace,
And on the gauzy network
    Their clumsy patterns trace,
Shut out the glorious sunlight,
    The breezy hills and glades,
And o'er the gleaming crystal
    Draw down their painted shades.

My own secluded chamber,
    On mountain slopes apart,
My deftly hidden loophole,
    Boasts no such studied art ;
'Tis but on windy mornings,
    In silver-sheeted rains,
I draw the blinds together,
    Replace the tiny panes.

And yet no glare of daylight
    My little nest invades,
No curious eye can spy it,
    Or pierce its chequered shades,

For I, too, have a curtain
  Of clearest, deepest green ;
More fine than satin damask
  Its texture and its sheen.

Fresh tendrils, closely clinging,
  Its loose, light fabric bind,
A net of twisted branches,
  A bower of leaves behind ;—
A golden gleam of sunlight,
  A breath of cooling air,
A snatch of happy music
  Await my presence there.

Between the leafy arches
  I gaze on new delight,
On mountain slopes of grandeur,
  On meadows daisy-white ;—
Let others drape their windows
  In silks and gauzes fine,
Of all their costly curtains
  Not one can rival mine.

LOVE'S IMAGE.

GAZE in thine eyes, my darling,
Gaze deep in thy lovely eyes,—
I see the light of thy girlish grace,
Of tear and smile a vanishing trace,
Thy dreamy fancies, thy thoughts refined,
The depth and strength of thy noble mind ;
Yet, deepest of all, thro' the quivering maze
I pierce with an earnest, steady gaze,
O deepest of all, my image lies
In the pure, true calm of thy speaking eyes !

I search thro' thy heart, my darling,
Search deep thro' thy loving heart,—
I see all charity for thy kind,
All wide and liberal thought I find,
I see thy tenderness, pure and free,
Thy faithful friendship and sympathy ;
Yet, deepest of all, 'mid the sacred flame
That kindles thy cheeks with a glowing shame,
O deepest of all, enshrined apart,
My image lies in thy constant heart !

I gaze in thine eyes, my darling,
Gaze deep in thy lustrous eyes,
And their passionate fervor thrills my brain,
Thrills with a bliss that is half a pain !
Clear, dilating, with tremulous grace
They mirror the rapture that lights my face :
I lift my head, no image lies
In the wondrous depths of thy liquid eyes,—
But if we meet, or if we part,
It is graven deep on thy faithful heart !

TRANSPLANTED.

PON the velvet carpet of the grass,
  Wrought close, and thick, and soft, a living
    green,
She lay ; a lithe, slight figure, finely formed,
Fashioned in supple grace and slender strength.
A rustic sun-bonnet, of faded brown,
Half hid her rippling wealth of chestnut hair,
Shading the dreamy gaze of liquid eyes,
Blue as the skies, and clear and deep as they,
With all their changefulness and constancy.
Her soft complexion, tho' by nature fair,
Tanned by the warm sun to a riper brown
That only deepened, as it could not hide
The mantling color that would oft suffuse
The smooth, transparent texture of her skin.
A pair of red lips, soft and fresh and fine,
And sensitive to every ruder breath
Or deep emotion.   Simple, yet intense
The clear-cut outlines of her youthful face.

The sun-bonnet that o'er her head was thrown,
Bounded the small, yet limitless extent
Of her horizon :—one fair bit of sky,
A cloudless sky of pure and perfect blue,
One silken tuft of grass, one modest flower,
One vagrant bee that murmured in its cup,
And a few scattered ears of ripening grain,
That rippled into golden wealth beyond ;
With summer sunshine brooding over all.
On these she gazed, and ever as she gazed,
Her blue eyes widened with an eagerness
Betraying the deep yearnings of her soul,
The doubtful wish that long had stirred her heart.
She longed, but knew not that for which she longed,
That larger life, that fuller harmony,
Was near her heart and ready to her hand.
Her country life to her seemed poor and mean
Because so grandly simple.   Restlessly
She beat against imaginary wires,
Seeking for what the world calls freedom ; not
The grand, pure freedom, sacred liberty,
Of Nature on her mountain heights, alone.
No ! still she dreamed her life's young, foolish dream
Of mighty cities and of mighty men,
And fancying in the great, cold, outside world,
Her larger feelings might find larger vent,
With sudden fervor she resolved to go.

And so she went : to try a city life,—
In fruitless toil and dreary dullness, drain
The living fonts of peace and purity,
From mother Nature's generous bosom drawn.
Her foot, that lightly pressed the sloping sward,
Climbed the rough crag, or thrid the tangled wood,
Robbed of its careless, graceful freedom, trod
But heavily o'er pavements smooth and hard.
Her ear, accustomed to no harsher sound
Than song of bird, or bubble of the brooks,
Tired of the city's rude, unceasing noise,—
The horse-cars, grinding, grinding on the rails,
The voices, voices, voices everywhere !
Her eye, to tender, peaceful landscapes wont,
Grew weary, with a dull, continual pain,
Of her horizon, bounded by the high
Red walls of brick, still dismally the same,
Bare, unrelieved and staring ugliness.
The petty, trading spirit of the town
But filled her with disgust.   Her innocent mind
Had little known of stern necessity,
And saw in it a greedy worldliness.
The squalor, dirt, and helpless misery,
Thrilled all her soul with pity so intense,
It bled almost to breaking for the griefs
She felt so deeply, yet could not assuage.
But oh ! the malice, scorn, the lies and thefts,

The deeds of conscious evil, worst of all !
Painfully foreign to her fresh young heart,—
So clear, and pure, and truthful in itself,
It had no room for dark suspicions, in
Its fearless trustfulness and innocence.
This were enough, and yet, behind it all,
A deeper, stranger trouble filled her breast.
She was a child of Nature.   She had lived
For twenty years in her secluded home,
And everything about or near it, lay
At her heart's core, and woven in her life.
She was a child of Nature from her birth :
Her heart and mind, her face and figure bore
The stamp of Nature's coinage.
                                    Frank and free,
Of steadfast truth, of simple piety,
Her passions glowed deep down in inner fires,
In fervid thoughts, strong and intense desires.
She felt her sad mistake, yet would not turn,
So firm the will beneath her slender frame,
Her sensitive and shrinking temperament,
The sense of pride, the tireless energy,
That bore her up when hope itself gave out.
So she staid on, and struggled on, and wore
Her young life to a dreary monotone.

How often thro' those long unhappy years,
The eye that beamed with hopeful eagerness,

Had quenched in bitter tears its youthful fires !
How often had that sweet and sensitive mouth
Quivered with deep emotion, all unshared,
And learned at last from hard experience,
The firm-set look of pain too closely kept !
The Spring could wake no hopes within her breast,
Of truer labor and of sweeter rest ;
The Summer had for her no joyous life,
The Autumn fields no golden harvest bore,
Nor purple fruitage mellowed to her hand ;
And cruel Winter, cold, and hard, and bare,
With bitter sharpness closed the dreary year.
Intent on work that brought no recompense,
She could or would not see where lay, for her,
The only field of simply true success.

At last the day of freedom dawned.   There came
An urgent message from her early home,
That called her back,—she could not choose but go,
Tho' almost dreading such a sudden rush
Of happy memories to her burdened heart.
But when she saw, above the sodden plain,
The blue soft outlines of her native hills,
When, slowly winding up the steep ascent,
The peaceful heavens high above her bent,
She saw the waving fields of ripened grain,
And heard the music of the shining rills,

The noble grandeur, perfect loveliness,
The power to thrill, to sanctify, to bless,
The breath of life, the influence divine,
Divinely gracious, bountiful and good,
Roused all the essence of her womanhood,—
She felt her slackened pulses quicker beat,
The warm blood started to her pallid cheek,
The old light flashed within her darkened eyes,
And, melted in a flood of happy tears,
One golden hour undid the work of years.

Upon the velvet carpet of the grass,
Wrought close, and thick, and soft, a living green,
She lay ; her girlish figure grown mature,
With well developed limbs and noble curves ;
Her massive co ls of hair still richly brown,
Tho' bright with less of sunshine than before ;
The same, yet not the same, her woman's face,—
Thro' its worn outlines shone a riper grace
Than careless youth and pleasure can bestow ;
Unlike the eager asking gaze of old,
Her eyes met yours with peaceful earnestness ;
A rich, deep color, fair as that which glows
Within the inmost bosom of the rose ;
A glorious Summer, strong in honest truth,
Replaced the blushful Spring of timid youth.

She rose, and with her blue eyes heavenward bent
In all the innate power of true intent,
With all the holy fervor of a prayer,
She breathed her soul upon the listening air :—
" Where Thou hast planted me, there let me stay,
My heart is here, here would I live and die,
And never turn my constant gaze away
From these green fields, and from this boundless sky.
My work is here, here will I ever strive
To use the precious gifts which Thou dost give ;
No vagrant hopes can tempt my soul to roam,
No place but this can ever be my home."

THE NINETEENTH OF JULY.

THE woods are clothed in deepest green,
    The fields are sweet with hay,
Cool breezes stir the sentient air
    And chase the heat away ;
The earth lies stretched in peaceful calm
    Beneath a cloudless sky,
Upon this bright midsummer day,—
    The nineteenth of July.

The year is at its zenith now,
    The earth is in its prime,
Search from the tropics to the poles,
    You'll find no fairer clime ;
Upon this breezy mountain height,
    'Tis ne'er too hot or dry,
But rich, and clear, and warm, and bright,—
    The nineteenth of July.

Yet thoughts and mem'ries dearer far
    Enrich these festal hours ;
The smiles and kisses they provoke

Are sweeter than the flowers ;
Glad children " Happy Birthday ! " call—
    Repeat the joyous cry!
It is the birthday of us all,—
    The nineteenth of July.

O mother dear, we vow it here,
    We would that we could bring
The harvest gold of half the world,
    Our birthday offering !
Yet if you will but take in love
    What time and wealth deny,
You still shall have a happy day
    This nineteenth of July.

JEWELS.

HE earth is a glorious jewel, deep set in the
      vastness of space,
  In the burnished gold of the sunlight, or the
    beams of the silver moon,
Girt round by an arch of sapphire, of a pure and
    constant grace,
  Suffused with the flush of dawning, or lost in an
    amber gloom.

The emerald slopes of summer are quick with the
    power they know,
  And the flowers shine like gems with a lustre
    purely bright ;
The whole wide earth seems fused in a passionate
    ruby glow,
  With a jewel's prisoned power, and a jewel's
    scatter'd light.

The crystal shine of Winter is clear and chaste as a
    pearl—
  As the shimmering rows of pearls that droop
    from the ice-bound sprays ;

Or a dazzling gleam of sunlight looks down thro' the
  toss and whirl,
  And the cold white crust is shivered with a
    thousand diamond rays.

The soul is a glorious jewel, in a wonderful setting
  run ;
  They're the same vibrating pulses that quicken
    and stir the whole ;
Jewel and setting together, they quiver and beat as
  one,
  For 'tis only thro' the setting that we may see the
    soul.

And some have souls like rubies, intense in a living
  glow,
  Strong to conquer and save, in a deep and fervid
    might ;
And some whose brilliant intellect has none of the
  heart's warm flow,
  Are like diamonds, clear and cold, flashing out
    a dazzling light.

Some burn like the fiery opal, now kindling into a
  flame,
  Now dying down to the embers, yet quick with a
    changeful gleam ;

Full of artistic spirit, that spirit never the same,
    Living half in a sharp reality, and half in a
    vivid dream.

And some have the strength of the ruby, its strength
    and constancy,
    With the frankness of the emerald, and the soft-
    ness of the pearl ;
These shine like radiant sapphires, with Faith and
    Charity,
    Beyond the common ignorance, above the common
    whirl.

Yet all are flawed and tarnished, and none are
    sound and whole,
    Blurred by sorrow and sin are the brightest and
    best of them ;
Here is a handsome face that stands for an empty
    soul,
    There from a broken setting there beams a
    beauteous gem.

O Father ! when Earth and her jewels are scat-
    tered to dust and decay,
    When the hearts which beat warm in our bosoms
    yearn upward and pant to be free,

Then pity our weakness and dullness, and gather
   Thy jewels, we pray,
     O. gather them into Thy casket and keep them
      forever with Thee !

There all shall be polished and perfect, and pure
   of all tarnish and stain,
     Untrammelled by physical struggle, where sick-
      ness and sorrow are o'er ;
There, set in the light of Thy presence, afar from
   earth's anguish and pain,
     May the jewels which Thou hast created shine
      bright with Thy love evermore !

THISTLES AND ROSES.

UPON the rugged mountain side,
 Uplifted in majestic pride ;
A squalid hovel stands ;
Of aspect rude, and harsh, and bare,
No fireside fancies cluster there
Of cultured thought and tender care,
 Warm hearts and loving hands.

The shrunken boards are black with rains ;
Old rags supply the missing panes ;
 The unhinged gate swings low,
And loosely hangs the clinking latch ;
Beyond, a shed of roughest thatch,
And ragged, cramped potato patch,
 The farmer's labor show.

A bank of thistles, prickly red,
A large and lusty burdock bed,
 The dingy yard adorn ;
A clump of daisies, run to seed,

And many a coarse, ill-favored weed,
With broken dishes—rude indeed,—
    A garden all forlorn !

Ten years pass by.   Upon the hill
The home of man is standing still,
    But oh how great a change !
Poised lightly on the wooded crest,
It fronts the sunset-painted west,
And breaks with outline picturesque
    The dusky, rolling range.

Of graceful form, of mellow tone ;
The generous windows, open thrown,
    Show curtains floating white ;
The porch above the sunny door,
The ivied lattice peeping o'er,
The rustic gate that stands before,
    More near approach invite.

The velvet lawn, well kept, tho' small,
Is skirted by a low, broad wall
    Where bright nasturtiums cling ;
Here bloom red roses, dewy wet,
And beds of fragrant mignonette,
In glowing gardens, richly set
    With many a lovely thing.

There purple pansies, quaint and low,
Forget-me-nots and violets grow,
  Or stately lilies shine;
Geraniums, vivid white and red,
Frail, bright-hued poppies, lightly shed,
And clasping, clinging, overhead,
  Long wreaths of tangled vine.

A light foot threads the fragile bowers,
Two slender hands are filled with flowers,
  A fair face all aglow ;
A soft smile curves the rosy lips,
To round red cheeks a dimple slips,
In liquid eyes the glad light dips,—
  She loves her garden so !

Poor hut, a blot on nature's face,—
And cottage quaint, of cultured grace,—
  A contrast sadly wide !
And wider still, 'twixt beds of bloom,
Of lustrous light, or softened gloom,
And unkempt yard of scanty room,
  With weeds on either side.

Yet widest 'twixt those hearts alone,
Where such pure light has never shone,
  And hearts abloom, aglow :

O may the happier lot be ours,
To live, not with, but thro' our flowers,
That soothe our griefs, inspire our powers,—
    Because we love them so !

TWIN LAKES—WAUSHINING.

LIGHT on the velvet turf I lie,
    'Twixt emerald earth and sapphire sky,
Soft-shaded 'neath the spreading trees,
And fanned by every shifting breeze.

A crystal mirror, finely set
In mountains dreamy violet,
    The lake's broad bosom meets my view,
As pure as fair, and fair as true.

Across the waters, soft, serene,
An island lifts its line of green ;
    Beyond its point the white sails fly,
And fishing boats at anchor lie.

In early morn how still it lies !
A faint blue haze 'neath hazy skies,
    Hushed in a languid light, to seem
A dreaming life a living dream.

At noon it takes a varying hue
Of beryl green, or liquid blue,
And glistening lower, and glancing higher,
It flashes up its silver fire.

Towards night the white clouds denser grow,
And from their caves the wild winds blow,
And heaving swell, and rippling tide,
O'er sea-green waters sinuous glide.

Thro' wind and wave the quick drops fall,
The veil of mist is over all,
Thro' flash and peal the dimples play,
The whirling eddies lashed to spray.

Night comes ; clouds break, and clear the way
For parting signal-lights of Day,—
The lake's calm peace is ours once more—
One mantling blush from shore to shore.

THE DEATH OF SUMMER.

HERE'S a break, there's a pause
  In the Earth's subtlest laws,
Since her fingers relaxed from their hold ;
  There's a chill in the air,
  Since the Form lying there
Grew suddenly rigid and cold.

  There's a dark shadow lies
  On the blue of the skies,
Since the light of her eyes last eclipse ;
  There's a clasp on the tongue,
  Since the songs that she sung
Were locked with the smile on her lips.

  'Tis the lapse of an hour,
  Ere a newly crowned power
Shall take up the year's broken thread ;
  She'll withhold the warm glow
  Of the presence we know,
And her cheeks' hectic flush give instead.

Not with clear, steady light
Will she dazzle our sight,
But with one brilliant flash of her eye ;
    And, too late, we may find
    We have left life behind,
And *her* life is but learning to die.

    But till then, O till then,
    Let us weep while we can,
Let us weep for the flower of the tomb ;
    For the red rose of day
    That has faded away,
Ere the gentian is fairly in bloom !

    Let us weep for the hair
    That is silvered with care ;
For the cheek that is hollow and wan ;
    For the worn look that lies
    In the heavy-fringed eyes ;
For the love and the life that are gone.

    For the false color weep
    That will kindle that cheek ;
The false light that will flash in that eye ;
    For the false flame that burns
    Till to ashes it turns,
And thus teaches Death how to die.

For the *year* that is dead,
Are the tears which we shed
When June and her roses decay ;
And if Summer departs
From the staunchest of hearts,
Its life-blood is ebbing away.

So we'll close up our eyes,
That no light on them rise
Since the light of her eyes last eclipse ;
And we'll tear out our tongue
For the songs we have sung,
And die with her smile on our lips.

———

O loosely swings the purpling vine,
The yellow maples flame before,
The golden-tawny ash trees stand
Hard by our cottage door :
October glows on every cheek,
October shines in every eye ;
While up the hill and down the dale
Her crimson banners fly !

VISIONS OF AUTUMN.

SEPTEMBER.

RANCED in a liquid calm September lies,
    Her bosom heaves with breathings soft and
        slow ;
The palpitating air in heart-warm stillness dies,
    And brooding peace is over all below.

The soft, thick tresses of her auburn hair
    Fall, richly massed, about her shapely head ;
Her heavy lashes lie dead black against
    A cheek of olive, quickened with fine red.

Or when she lifts her luminous blue eyes,
    A dreamy languor every sense pervades ;
The ripe lips melt in dewy tenderness,
    With thrice the nameless charm of earthly maids.

In simple russet clad, her kirtle laced
    With dextrous broidery of the pallid fern,
A twist of wild clematis round her waist,—
    Clasped in her tender palm bright blossoms burn.

Blow softly, wind, nor ruffle that rich hair !
　　Shine warmly, sun, on those ambrosial lips !
Hush ! break not yet that blest repose, nor dare
　　With darksome shadows that chaste light eclipse.

The soft south wind a russet drift has heaped ;
　　The faint south wind in drowsy murmur dies :
O would no wintry chill might ever reach
　　Where, tranced in liquid calm, September lies !

OCTOBER.

Quick with the breath of life, October stands,
　　For freedom, strength and vigor, past compare :
In queenly state she rules her forest lands,
　　Where maples light with flame the frosty air.

In fine loose ringlets falls her chestnut hair,
　　And clusters round her frank, undaunted brow ;
Her eager, earnest eyes are quick and keen,
　　Thro' all their tender depths of gentian blue.

The pure rich blood that mantles in her cheek,
　　Stains her full lips with crimson warm and clear ;
Her gracious, generous smile itself is seal
　　And guerdon of a golden harvest year.

In careless, yet most bright and brave attire ;
  A kirtle, golden brown and olive green,
A tawny yellow jacket fringed with fire,
  A sweeping mantle with a purple sheen.

Blow softly, wind ! one rude or reckless breath
  Might take from out her hair its silken flow ;
One dash of rain might drown those brave blue eyes,
  And drain from cheeks and lips their living glow.

The soft south wind hath flown unheeding by,
  And swept away across her forest lands :
O would no ice-bound spell might ever lie
  Where, quick with instant life, October stands !

NOVEMBER.

Wrung with a barren grief, November lies,
  An angry tumult raging in her brain,
Catching her broken breath in shuddering sighs,
  With clenched hands, tossing in convulsive pain.

A dull dead brown her strands of flying hair,
  In withered heaps of loose confusion piled,
Her great blue eyes fixed in a glassy stare,
  Have vacant, dumb expression, sad and wild.

Her hollow cheeks are haggard, pale and wan,
    Her white set mouth no woful word can frame.
From cold stiff limbs all sense of life is gone,
    She lies bereft, in numb unconscious pain.

A shroud of gloomy grey about her thrown,
    Shields her slight form from Autumn's nipping air,
The pale witch-hazel's scattered light alone
    Falls on the brow that once we knew so fair.

Blow, bitter wind ! in bitter anguish mourn !
    Wail, shriek and wail thy weird and mystic grief !
Till lightly on the whirling gust upborne,
    Flutters and falls the last forsaken leaf.

The keen northwind hath fainted at her feet,
    And breathed its burdened heart in weary sighs :
O would no sharper blast might ever reach
    Where, tranced in rigid calm, November lies !

THANKSGIVING.

CROSS the grey November sky,
  The damp, dense clouds are drifting,
Between the branches, bare and high,
  The powdery snow is sifting;
In sheltered hollows, withered leaves
  In sodden heaps are lying,
And underneath our vine-hung eaves
  The weary wind is sighing.

Then why thro' all the misty air
  These clarion church bells pealing?
Why brings this dull day everywhere
  Glad bursts of grateful feeling?
Why, why are all the pantry shelves
  With fruity richness teeming?
And whence these spicy-odored pies,
  So crisp and tender seeming?

Wisely and well, in earlier times,
  This happy day was chosen,
That tho' the earth grow stiff and bare,
  Our hearts might not be frozen;

That fall by fall, and year by year,
   Kind words know no declining,
The wilder storm, the warmer cheer,
   Where light of love is shining.

When Spring leaps forth in wood and field,
   Then eager hearts are springing !
When Autumn doth her harvest yield,
   What rapture marks the bringing !
'Tis bliss enough on Summer days,
   The blind delight of living ;
A higher joy must thrill our hearts,
   To make a true Thanksgiving.

When every venture prospers well,
   And every wish is granted,
When constant sunshine seems to dwell
   O'er souls unchilled, undaunted,
The fountains of a grateful love,
   In grateful hearts are welling,
The free, unbidden song of praise,
   Full melody is swelling.

But when dark clouds obscure our day,
   And gathering troubles sadden,
When, plodding on our weary way,
   We find no hope to gladden,

Then comes the test of thankfulness,
  Then comes the sharpest trial,
When faith alone can overcome
  A cold and hard denial!

O! let us hold unruffled still
  The pure peace of believing;
The clear, rich anthem of our praise
  Be free from notes of grieving;
In sweet, serene and thankful hearts
  Lies all the joy of living;—
Lift pure and strong your choral song,
  And make a glad Thanksgiving!.

THE FARM BEYOND THE HILLS.

REEN in the meadow the grass upspringing,
 Clear thro' the woodlands the birds' glad
  singing,
Fresh young life to the cold earth bringing,
  Ripple the bubbling rills ;
Strong and ardent the Summer's glowing ;
Wan and withered the Autumn's going ;
Wild and wintry the cold storm beating,—
But all slip by like a shadow fleeting
  O'er the Farm beyond the Hills.

Sunlight dazzles and tempests shiver,
Strong is the action of wind and weather,
Earth's finest fibres to scorch and sever
  With the might of many wills ;
But the Frost King's breath like a breath is over,
And the veils of cloud but a moment cover,
And the passionate glow of a noontide burning
Leaves but the languor of distant yearning,
  On the Farm beyond the Hills.

With the dewy roses of day-dawn flushing ;
Thro' the limpid air of the morning blushing ;
While the amber wave of sunset gushing,
        A softened glory distills ;
In melted amethyst mantling, fainting;
With pearls and sapphires the cold sky painting ;
In a far-off dream of blue light dying;
Yet still with an unchanged grandeur lying
        On the Farm beyond the.Hills.

Older than ruin and rust of ages,
Wiser and purer than saints and sages,
It stands where the rattle of rude life rages,
        Yet the realm of fancy fills ;
Forever constant, and true, and tender,
Forever grand in its stately splendor,
Forever chaste in its curves sublime,
Thro' the depth of distance and flow of time,
        Is the Farm beyond the Hills.

HAPPY BIRTHDAY : A TWO-FOLD SONG.

I. C. C.
R. S. G.

DEC. 14TH, 1877.

HERE'S twice the greetings two have known,
 With twice the ardor lent to one,
In double measure, doubly done,
  We wish you Happy Birthday !

Ring out your voices twice as clear
As two could make them, twice a year,
Bring twice the love and twice the cheer,
  To this twice Happy Birthday !

What double tasks to me belong,
With two to swell the twice-told wrong !
How shall I twist my two-fold song,
  To suit this Happy Birthday ?

May twice the joys of man below,
Be yours to share and yours to know,

With two-fold radiance may they glow
    Thro' many a Happy Birthday!

May two fast friends, where'er they meet,
This day with two-fold gladness greet,
And two dear lives be made twice sweet,
    Each doubly Happy Birthday!

Tho' twice as shrill the wild winds blow,
And doubly deep the cold white snow,
No storm can chill the two-fold glow
    That lights this Happy Birthday.

Then twice the greetings two have known,
With twice the ardor lent to one ;
In double measure, doubly done,
    We wish you Happy Birthday!

ROSE LEAVES.

HE crimson petals of the Rose,
  In glowing hues how richly dressed !
How doth each regal bloom disclose
  A mantling blush, a warm unrest !

But when the worn and withered flower
  Is of her royal robes bereft,
How passing sweet her lasting dower !
  How pure, how rich the fragrance left !

So may this glad and glowing day,
  Full lightly poised on restless wing,
With eager welcome speed away,
  And rosy greetings blushing bring.

Then, when the golden sun is set,
  And phantom hours glide softly by,
May breath of roses haunt us yet,
  From scattered leaves of Memory.

CHRISTMAS CAROL.

BURN, Christmas lights, burn chaste and clear !
  Blaze out against the stormy sky,
From windows warm with Christmas cheer,
  And rosy tapers flaming high !
All sparkling, glowing greetings send,
From lip of love and heart of friend,
And bear to those who grieve alone,
Glad tidings sent to every one.

Peal, Christmas bells, peal loud and deep !
  Ring out a merry Christmas chime,
Till darkened eyes forbear to weep,
  And hard hearts glow with love divine :
In rippling music die away,
With ringing laughter glad and gay,
Till rich and full the dark night swells,
With Christmas lights and Christmas bells !

CHRISTMAS POEM.

THE GUIDING STAR.

SHADOWS close and darken round us ;
    Life is weary, time is long ;
Thro' the beating storms of winter,
    Pause, and listen to our song :
We are watchers on the mountains,
    Lonely, gazing near and far,
Watching for the promised glory,
    Waiting for the Guiding Star.

Whence shall come the light to cheer us ?
    Whither shall we wend our way ?
Summer's latest rose is faded,
    Gone the last faint flush of day ;
Who shall tell us where to labor,
    Strive in peace, or strike in war ?
Come, O Herald of Salvation !
    Come and lead us, Guiding Star !

Rising thro' the clear blue ether,
  In the azure depths of night ;
Shining with a holy lustre,
  Large and pure, and calm and bright ;—
Lo ! the Star, the Star of Morning,
  Thro' the blue depths seen afar !
Feast thine eyes upon its splendor,
  Gaze upon the Guiding Star !

Still it moves, it journeys onward,
  Over hill, and rock, and glen :
Rise and follow ! rise and follow !
  Waiting women, watching men !
Onward, swift as rushing rivers,
  Scale the crag and leap the scar,
Falter not, brave heart, and faint not,
  Follow fast the Guiding Star !

Ye that seek a kingly grandeur,
  Onward still, ye cannot stay !
Ye that boundless wealth would gather,
  Turn, and seek an easier way ;
But, O loving hearts and faithful,
  Following Jesus fast and far,
Pause and see, o'er yonder village,
  Rests at last the Guiding Star.

Haste thee to that humble manger,
    Lowly kneel, and meekly pray,
Till the blessing of the Savior
    Makes thy darkness light as day ;
While on angel's wings descending,
    Love unlocks the golden bar,
Touched, and quickened into being,
    Rise and thank the Guiding Star !

Heaven sheds all her rays about us ;
    Life is noble, truth is long ;
Thro' the beating storms of Winter,
    Pause, and listen to our song :
We are toilers in the conflict,
    Straining. struggling, near and far ;
Christmas-tide brings Christmas tidings,—
    We have found the Guiding Star !

ALL ROUND THE YEAR.

ALL round the year the sun shines bright,
    The pale moon sheds her softer light,
The day a brilliant beauty shows,
The night in drowsy stillness goes:
The massive links of mountain chains,
The dimpled swells of fertile plains,
The boughs of trees, the roots of flowers,
    At least, are always here;
And Nature keeps her sacred powers
    All round the year.

All round the year the brave hearts beat,
The ruddy limbs are strong and fleet;
With youth and health the tokens lie,
Of glowing cheek and flashing eye;
No chilling influence need we know,
'Mid summer shine or winter snow;
Warm hands to clasp, warm lips to press,
    Warm friends, forever dear,
Warm life, and love and happiness
    All round the year.

All round the year the cultured mind
A higher culture still may find,
May press beyond the surging throng
With yearning deep and labor strong :
The star of Science knows no cloud,
The flower of Art no snow-cold shroud,
No season moves the busy brain,
    The brain that's strong and clear ;
With equal force we toil and strain
    All round the year.

All round the year the trusting soul
May find the word of promise whole ;
The eye of faith, once firmly stayed,
No doubt can move, no sorrow shade ;
The flight of time, unknown above,
Breaks not our Father's boundless love,
Unbroken be the tranquil light
    That folds our lesser sphere,
As ever pure, and calm, and bright,
    All round the year.

Then mourn not, friend, the cutting air,
The fields so white, the trees so bare ;
Let no false grief employ your tongue,
Nor wish the year forever young :

The flower must fade, the leaf must fall,
But one great Power is over all :
If, thro' the ceaseless round of change
    One changeless Will appear,
Unmoved, undaunted may we range
    All round the year.

A NEW YEAR'S GREETING.

THE music of Christmas is ebbing away,
 The blue of September has faded to grey,
The roses of June 'neath the snow-drifts are laid,
And in coinage of gold April's raindrops are paid.
 Then sing! for the Old Year has spent of his
  store,
 And sing to the New Year to bring us some
  more ;
 We crave his indulgence, we ask of his cheer,
 We wish you, we wish you a Happy New Year !

May the storm-winds of Winter pass light o'er your
  head,
May the breath of the may-flower be over you shed,
May the roses of Summer with love be aglow
Till the year is again wrapt in mantle of snow ;
 Then sing! for the Old Year has spent of his
  store,
 And sing to the New Year to bring us some
  more ;
 We crave his indulgence, we ask of his cheer,
 We wish you, we wish you a Happy New Year !

AN ICE STORM.

I.

ON wings of wind the wild March day flew by,
    Shrouded in floating mists and sleety rain;
And now the pale, cold light begins to wane,
Blown in grey waves across the gloomy sky :
Tho' safe within, we feel the tempest nigh :
    With bated breath, against the quivering pane,
    We gaze thro' all the seething storm again,
Where, white with frost, the naked meadows lie,
Where, limb on limb, the swaying forests stand,
    Their leafless branches tost in pearly spray ;
        A sea of crystal, crested high with foam,
In hissing waves sweeps o'er the ice-bound land ;
    Now pure and pale thro' fainting lights of day,
        Now lost in stormy gloom when night is come

II.

All night keen winds have scourged the frosty plain ;
  All night the groaning boughs have clashed and
    swung ;
Now chaste and clear the morning breaks along
The still, cold glory wrought by wind and rain.
What wondrous grace a fettered limb may gain !
  Earth seems one grand, white flower, thro' tem-
    pests wrung,
  In perfect poise uplifted, drooped and hung,
With petals lily-curved and pure of stain.
The ground is ridged with crystal, every tree
  Bending and swaying, cased in glittering mail,
    And fringed with icicles the swinging vine ;
Winter's white radiance deepens dazzlingly ;
  Now milk-white pearls in shimmering crescents
    pale,
    Now flashing diamonds light her crystal
    shrine.

BEAUTY FOR ASHES.

"Give unto them beauty for ashes."—ISAIAH LXI. 3.

THE fire of Home is burning low,
    The sunken flames relax their mirth,
The dying embers faintly glow,
    And ashes strew the barren hearth ;
Breathe soft ! the hot coals flush for shame ;
    The smoking brands together press,
Till leap the writhing tongues of flame
    In wild, fantastic loveliness.

The fire of Joy is burning low,
    No fuel given whereon to feed,
Pale ashes quench its ruddy glow,
    To eat the heart in time of need ;
Yet night precedes a brighter day,
    Pain brings a bliss more pure and high,
Where, underneath this shroud of grey
    In undimmed light red rubies lie.

The fire of Love is burning low,
    Low on the heart's wide hearthstone laid,
O'er the red coals pale ashes grow,
    Strange symbols of a beauteous dead ;
Yet breathe warm gusts of living truth,
    The quick flames leap aloft once more,
New ardor, kindling warm as youth,
    Its fervent glow shall yet restore.

The fire of Life is burning low !
    Cold grows the hand once strong and warm,
Life's bright and beaming symbols go
    From ashen cheek and shrunken form ;
Yet, tho' the quivering flame be still,
    God's kindling breath shall bid it rise,
In waves of living light to thrill,
    And blaze triumphant in the skies.

FAITH, HOPE AND LOVE.

THE bulrush grows at the water's brim
   While its pennons fringe the mere,
So grows my Faith in the soil of Earth,
   Yet blooms in a higher sphere.

The lily creeps from the cool, damp mould
   And floats on the lake's calm breast,
So my Hope doth bloom thro' the darkest gloom
   In a pure and peaceful rest. .

But the water cradles and rocks them all,
   And bubbles and breaks above,
So pure, so deep, in its shimmering sweep,
   Is the ocean of my Love.

WELCOME SPRING.

BRIGHT and breezy, brave and clear,
    Strong new life in every vein,
March begins the rolling year,
    Starts anew the wild refrain :—
Hark ! the cool winds fresher blow ;
Hark ! the clear streams freer flow ;
Hark ! the birds exultant sing,—
        Welcome, Spring !

Moist and brown the naked sod,
    Quick'ning to an olive green,
Streaked with snow, that lingers still
    Where the sheltering fences lean ;
Higher, lines of trees that stand
Stiff and bare, on either hand,
Murmuring, as they rock and swing,—
        Welcome, Spring !

On the blue hills far away,
    Hazy dreams of distance lie,
While white drifts of cloudland float
    O'er a clear and wind-blown sky ;

In the air a subtle power,
Faint, sweet breath of leaf and flower,
Thro' the damp mould whispering,—
    Welcome, Spring !

Once released from Winter's spell,
    Once his icy reign is o'er,
Shall our eager hearts rebel,
    Dashed against his desert shore?
Nay, for once the germ possessed,
Ours, in truth, are all the rest,
Flower and fruitage Time shall bring,—
    Welcome, Spring !

Bright and breezy, brave and clear,
    Strong new life in every vein,
March begins the rolling year,
    Starts anew the wild refrain :—
Hark ! the cool winds fresher blow ;
Hark ! the clear streams freer flow :
Hark ! the birds exultant sing,—
    Welcome, Spring !

S. H. W.

APRIL 23, 1878.

"A life that moves to gracious ends
Thro' troops of unrecording friends,
A deedful life, a silent voice."

THRO' all the doubtful April day,
　　A settled vapor fainting broods,
Cool breezes stir the silent woods,
Soft sunlight drives the clouds away.

The rarest bloom is close in bane :
　　The brightest ray has dreamy veil
　　Of Hope, far-seeing, pure and pale,
Of Memory, touched with tender pain.

Yet, from the dewy, hidden flowers
　　A wondrous fragrance fills the air ;
　　A chastened light, serenely fair,
Makes golden-clear the quiet hours.

And, spite of fitful wind and storm,
　　A stately grace, a tender calm,
　　For wounded hearts a gentle balm,
Makes the grey twilight deep and warm.

How strangely sweet her silent part,
  Whose pure, unselfish labor stirs
  Like wings of angel messengers
The secret fountains of the heart !

God bless her work, and such as hers,
  Who live in others' lives alone ;
  Increase the ever widening zone,
The sacred circle of her cares !

And when her heart shall cease to beat,
  Enshrined in painless peace above,
  Fill up the measure of her love,
And make the broken sphere complete !

WELCOME!

WINTER is over and gone,
   Gone with the frost and the snow,
With the streams that quiver,
The trees that shiver,
   The winds that bluster and blow.
Clasped in a mighty arm,
   Borne on a living wing,
Sprung from the earth, or fall'n from the skies,
   Welcome, our Flower of Spring!

Summer is yet to come,
   Her roses have yet to blow,—
Alike remote
From the warbling throat,
   And the winding-sheet of snow;
We gather the violet shy,
   The mayflower pale and lone,
For the sweet mid-spring
Our babe did bring,
   Afar from the Great Unknown.

Not ours are sorrow and care,
  All those with Winter have gone ;
Not ours the pleasure
Too full for measure,
  In the flush of a Summer's dawn ;
Our joy is token of more,
  We smile on the passing hour,
The fruit shall come in its own good time,—
  God has given the flower.

Then welcome to sweet Sky Farm !
  To song, and sunlight, and bloom,
For Love rejoices,
Thro' myriad voices,
  In acres of woodland room.
O, strange, mysterious birth !
  Thrilled with its power we sing,—
Welcome, our pure on earth !
  Welcome, our Flower of Spring !

NATURE'S COINAGE.

APROPOS OF THE BLAND SILVER BILL.

HRO' talk and trouble, shallow and strange,
We get our "medium of exchange;"
Tho' all are eager for money, you'll find
Each one must have his favorite kind.

"A tipsy senate passes the bill,—"
The papers quarrel about it still;
Silver or paper, is that the fuss?
If we only get some, it's one to us!

On the busy mart, or the crowded street,
Our stamp and seal are made complete;
There's a dingy ceiling, a grimy floor,
And a mine of wealth from door to door.

Nay! leave the town with its surge and strain,
From dollar to dollar, loss or gain,
And breathe the air of the breezy hill
Where all is tranquil, and pure and still.

'Tis true, for many a month and more
The wild winds fought for our scatter'd store,
And never a genuine coin was told
Since the last witchhazel's gleam of gold.

'Tis true old Winter was cold and stern,—
But he poured rare gems from his crystal urn,
With milk-white pearls his robe was set,
And diamonds flashed in his coronet.

Now Spring sweeps over the swaying wood,
In shafts of sunlight, and pillars of cloud ;
And shifting breeze, and pattering rain,
Sweet Nature's coinage renew again.

Ere the first flower creeps from the leafy mould
The bare black alders are fringed with gold,
And the silver buds are fair to see,
On the boughs of the slender willow tree.

The gold is ours ; we take and buy
A softer wind and a bluer sky ;
The silver slips from our hands, and lo !
The pink arbutus begins to blow.

But soon, too soon our April 's past,
With its shy, pale blossoms, too frail to last ;

The seal and guerdon of wealth untold
We clasp in the wild marsh-marigold.

Then leafy tangles of green are ours,
And clear-voiced birds, and bright-hued flowers,
Till the modest daisy brings Summer nigh,
With its silver petals and golden eye.

So, lightly fleeting, the Summer goes,
And fainting and fading her crimson rose ;
Soft music swells on the sentient air,
And the sweetest of incense is everywhere.

Now Autumn marshals her brilliant train,
With ripened fruitage and garnered grain,
And the golden-rod by the roadside waits
As entrance fee to her palace gates.

A moment—the forest drops its crown,
The leaves are rustling in withered brown,
And the witchhazel gleams thro' the woodlands
    drear,
The last pale gold of the dying year.

Man's intricate systems and dull debate,
His struggles for self and questions of " State "—
Such craft is bad and leads to worse,
A ruined life and an empty purse !

But Nature's coinage of fire and dew,
Is grandly simple and nobly true,
And all may purchase a richer wealth,
A fuller freedom, a stronger health,

A purer air, and a freer room,
A richer fruitage and brighter bloom,
A sounder life, serene and strong,
A fresher fancy, a sweeter song.

Then leave the town with its surge and strain
From dollar to dollar, loss or gain,
And over the hills where the stream runs clear
You may live full many a happy year.

GRANDFATHER'S BIRTHDAY.

C. G.

APRIL 24th, 1791—1878.

'TWAS many an April morn ago,
    Cooled by soft winds and gentle show·
      ers,
Vibrant with music clear and low,
    And drifted white with flowers.

On that blest day a son was given,
    A simple child of April's own,
With soul as fresh and pure from Heaven,
    As violets newly blown.

He lived thro' Summer's fervid glow,
    With brave resolve he joined the strife,
Yet still preserved the even flow,
    The tranquil beauty of his life.

He lived thro' Autumn's harvest hours,
    He gained what honest work achieves,
Yet bound his dewy April flowers
    Among his golden sheaves.

He lived thro' Winter's piercing blast,
   'Thro' storms of grief and clouds of care,
And still, with tranquil faith, held fast
   The buds he used to wear.

His are the fruits of kindly deeds ;
   The garnered grain of labor strong ;
The wisdom, strength, and love, that lead
   To lives so true and long.

Yet still, ah ! still these triumphs bring
   No signs of weakness or decay,—
He breathes the freshness of his spring
   Thro' Life's autumnal day !

An April morn is round us now,
   Cooled by soft winds and gentle showers,
Vibrant with music clear and low,
   And drifted white with flowers.

NEAREST HEAVEN.

THRO' the dear, familiar voices,
   Known and loved so well and long,
Framing words of strength and solace,
   Sober truth or happy song,
Comes a tone of subtler meaning,
   Strangely sweet and thrilling clear,
Sudden cry, or cooing murmur,
   Foreign to our duller ear.

All among the brave home faces,
   Bright and warm thro' lines of care,
Shows a still face, pure and perfect,
   Ringed about with shining hair ;
Lips unchilled, and brow undaunted,
   Gaze heaven-clear and angel-wise,
With a depth of tender meaning
   Far beyond our mortal eyes.

In our home, where light and longing
   Struggle sore thro' toil and strain,
Comes a presence, sweet and holy,
   Thro' Life's sacrament of pain ;

And a tender awe is blended
  With our love's protecting balm,
As we kiss the baby features,
  Nearest Heaven's immortal calm.

THE LADY'S-SLIPPER.

WHERE Cinderella dropped her shoe,
   'Tis said in fairy tales of yore,
'Twas first the lady's-slipper grew,
   And there its rosy blossom bore.

And ever since, in woodlands grey,
   It marks where Spring retreating flew,
Where, speeding on her eager way,
   She left behind her dainty shoe.

On pensile stem it drooping sways,
   Pale, pink-veined blossom, lightly swung,
Here, brushing thro' yon tangled ways,
   'Twas lost these withered leaves among.

Like Prince of old, on romance bent,
   We bring it home with tender care ;
But all in vain—the magic lent
   By fairy lore still lingers there.

Yet see, alas! no foot we find
   To fit that shoe so slender-small :
Our Cinderella's left behind,—
   So let her lady's-slipper fall.

LILY AND ROSEBUD.

LILY and Rosebud bloom together,
    All in the garden beds of home ;
Hearts close-prest thro' the darkest weather,
    All together they bud and bloom ;
Lily drooping, and white, and slender,
Rosebud dewy, and pink, and tender,
Hearts love-warm thro' the coldest weather
    Close together they bud and bloom.

TO ————

THE dewy light of early morn
   Hath melted from thy skies,
The transient flush that breaks the dawn
   Is lost in sapphire blue ;
But noon's full calm, like burnished gold
   Across thy pathway lies,
A stronger light, a deeper glow,
   Than careless childhood knew.

The fragile bloom of tender Spring
   Hath vanished from thy sight,
The birds no longer trill their notes
   With such unconscious glee ;
But look where royal roses burn,
   Where gracious fruits hang ripe,
And round the watchful parent birds
   Their downy nestlings see.

Then why, dear heart, should darkling eve
   Cast shades of night before ?
Or Winter lay his icy hand
   On Summer's warmest glow ?

Nay, bask within thy fuller light,
 Enjoy thy riper store,
Nor lay thy purple mantle down
 For drifting robes of snow !

THROUGH STORM AND CALM.

WANDERING wind ! why pause and falter
    now ?
Why check the freedom of thy wild refrain ?
This white, oppressive silence weighs me down,
    And chills my life-blood with a stagnant pain.

O shy, pale flower, in dewy stillness hid,
    Break from thy bonds and greet the living sky ;
Lift the dark fringes of thy quivering lid,
    And light the forest with thine azure eye!

Winter is gone, his rudest storms are past,
    Then why, O why should happy spring delay ?
Burst into sunshine, gloomy sky, at last,
    Roll on the zenith of unclouded day !

This hushed suspense beseems not such an hour,
    My heart beats warmly and the winds are dumb ;
Nay, if we still are held in Winter's power
    Break the dead pause, and bid the tempest come!

From distant hills, lost in a dream of blue,
    From tossing mists, and floating, pale-gray skies,

From meadows olive green, and dark brown wood,
  In accents soft and low a Voice replies :—

"Canst thou not wait ?   The years may come and
    go,
  Yet count them not : Eternity is thine ;
Life has its hours of steady ebb and flow ;
  Years break like waves against the shores of Time.

"Winter is gone, his rudest storms are past,
  Why wouldst thou grasp at once the Summer's
    rose ?
This hour of sweet probation may not last,—
  Taste its pale joys, accept its soft repose.

"Winter is gone, yet Summer is not here,
  And blinding storms may yet await thee there :
Why wouldst thou meet an unknown grief too near,
  For which these quiet moments may prepare ?"

Nay, gentle Voice, they may be sweet to thee,
  Too pure and calm to burn with human fire ;
Empty of promise, they are filled by me
  With torturing fear and passionate desire.

I cannot follow out a growth so slow ;
  My thoughts outrun the goal ere yours begin :

This moment was exhausted long ago,
  And chilled without, I burn and glow within.

Still, from far hills, lost in a dream of blue ,
  Still, from soft winds, and floating, pale-grey skies,
Divinely calm, serenely pure and true,
  In accents grave and clear a Voice replies :—

"Return, and follow back the steps repassed,
  Too hot haste misses what it fain would find ;
We speed the circle round, and pause at last,
  Wearied and worn, to find ourselves behind.

"Canst thou not wait ?   This hour of silent rest,
  So pure, so still, untouched by pain or strife,
May farther reach than toil unduly pressed,
  And all be just, for all is in a life.

"With one great object evermore in view,
  Thro' storm and calm the varying years may roll ;
Why ask for strife—a warrior brave and true ?
  Why crave for rest if peace be in thy soul ?"

———

On distant hills, lost in a dream of blue,
  I gaze, at last, with perfect peace possessed ;
Thro' rest and toil my Guide is ever true :
  I wait, meanwhile, the Land where all is rest.

TWO SONNETS.

I.

BABY.

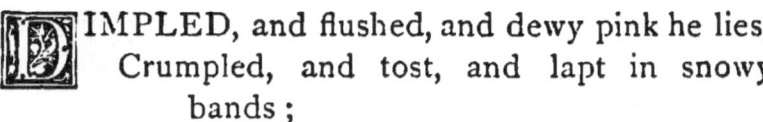IMPLED, and flushed, and dewy pink he lies,
 Crumpled, and tost, and lapt in snowy
  bands ;
 Aimlessly reaching with his tiny hands,
Lifting in wondering gaze his great blue eyes.
Sweet, pouting lips, parted by breathing sighs ;
 Soft cheeks, warm-tinted as from tropic lands ;
 Framed with brown hair in shining, silken strands,—
All fair, all pure, a sunbeam from the skies !
O perfect innocence ! O soul enshrined
 In blissful ignorance of good or ill,
  By never gale of idle passion crossed !
Altho' thou art no alien from thy kind,
 Tho' Pain and Death may take thee captive still,
  Thro' Sin, at least, thine Eden is not lost !

II.

MOTHER.

Upon her snowy couch she drooping lies,
   A languor on her limbs that seems a grace,
   A sacred pallor on her lily face,
A blessed light reflected in her eyes.
She knows who drew her strength and would not rise;
   Forgetting self, she rests a little space,
   Sees her warm life-blood mantle in his face,
And strains her ear to catch his wailing cries.
O wondrous mother-love ! how strange, and deep
   With what vibrating thrill of tenderness !
     To give the glow, and lie a pallid flower !
To give the light, and smile, and wait to weep !
   Sweet is thine infant's warm unconsciousness,
     But sweeter thy mysterious sacred power.

In Memoriam.

E. R.

AUGUST 10, 1878.

THREE SONNETS.

I.

ON THE BRINK.

ALL night we watched beside her dying bed,
    All night we paced her hushed and dark-
        ened room,
Thro' the deep stillness and the holy gloom
We knelt, to catch the halo round her head.
Could that faint breath ere break of day be fled,
    That fair, calm face its last sweet sleep resume,
    Those still, white hands lie folded for the tomb,
And yet the love that moved them be not dead ?
When, faint and blind, to the wide air we stole,
    Our sobs were strangled in the abyss of Heaven,
        Whose clear, dark blue was lanced with silver
            beams—

That grand, chaste splendor stilled the anguished
    soul !
  With angel wings the starry vault was riven,
    Bearing pure spirits to unbroken dreams.

II.

AT PEACE.

A still, clear day, a tranquil August noon ;
  Deep peace, full calm, on all the drowsy air ;
  Soft, brooding warmth on the shorn grainfields,
    where
Lies a rich harvest, Heaven's most precious
    boon.
We grieve not that our wheat was reaped so soon ;
  'Tho' its broad emerald waves were passing
    fair.
  These golden sheaves a fuller meaning bear,
And August brings a riper bliss than June.
Thus calmly muse on this still face serene,
  This life fulfilled in love, and closed in peace,
    Unscarred by passion, perfect grown thro' pain;
We loved her,--learned on her sweet life to lean,--
  Yet dare not mourn that such a life should
    cease
    When the Great Reaper takes His ripened
    grain.

III.

BEYOND.

Still, night will come,—a night of doubts and fears !
  Gone, she is gone ! and never, never more
  Her gentle smile shall greet us at the door.:—
We sink beside it drowned in hopeless tears !
O aching Past ! O blinding weight of years !
  O dim and distant, on the heavenly shore,
  We need thy saintly presence borne before,
To guard and guide us till the Light appears !
Yet, if she lives, ours is not wholly loss :
  —The yearning heart that none can satisfy,
  The empty chair that no one else can fill—
Her sweet, strong influence lifts our heavy cross ;
  Touched with the benison of her memory,
    Encompassed by her love, we have her still !

POEMS.

-

DORA READ GOODALE.

BORN, *Oct. 29th*, 1866.

SPRING AND SUMMER.

IN Spring we note the breaking
　　Of every baby bud,
In Spring we note the waking
　　Of wild flowers of the wood ;
In Summer's fuller power,
　　In Summer's deeper soul,
We watch no single flower,
　　We see, we breathe the whole !

WAIT.

WHEN the icy snow is deep,
    Covering the frozen land,
Do the little flowerets peep
    To be crushed by Winter's hand!

No, they wait for brighter days,
    Wait for bees and butterflies,
Then their dainty heads they raise
    To the sunny, sunny skies.

When the cruel north winds sigh,
    When 'tis cold with wind and rain,
Do the birdies homeward fly
    Only to go back again?

No, they wait for Spring to come,
    Wait for gladsome sun and showers,
Then they seek their northern home,
    Seek its leafy, fragrant bowers.

Trustful as the birds and flowers,
   Tho' our spring of joy be late,
Tho' we long for brighter hours,
   We must ever learn to wait.

A WELCOME TO BABY MARTHA.

O WHAT tho' the wild winds are blowing so
    shrill
  And an icy cold hand on our darling they lay,
O what tho' the snowflakes still give us a chill
    As they fall, and they fall, and they melt not
        away !

The last day of March when the robins were sing-
    ing,
  Were singing their joy that the grasses were green,
I heard the winds whisper the woods should be
    ringing
  With praise to their Queen, to their new baby
        Queen.

And then all the robins they poured forth a welcome,
  And the sun it smiled down on her sweet baby
      grace,
And I joined in the welcome, the glad, happy
    welcome,
  Which made the woods ring in the depth of their
      space.

O may she be sweet as the heart-cheering sunshine,
  That shone on her cradle so soft and so low,
And may she be bright as the beautiful blossoms,
  As glad as the birds and as pure as the snow !

DARK THE DAY, BUT BRIGHT THE HEART.

DARK the day but bright the heart,
  True, true friends can never part,
Cold the storm and dark the day,—
We can love, and love alway.

Tho' the winds should moan and cry,
Tho' they wearily should sigh,
Love can shed a gladsome ray,—
We can love, and love alway.

Then, when Springtime's happy bloom
Sheds about a rich perfume,
Love's sweet harvest ours that day,
We will love, and love alway.

SUMMER IS COMING.

"SUMMER is coming!" the soft breezes
        whisper,
"Summer is coming!" the glad birdies sing,
Summer is coming! I hear her quick footsteps,—
    Take your last look at the beautiful Spring!

Lightly she steps from her throne in the woodlands,—
    "Summer is coming, and I cannot stay;
Two of my children have crept from my bosom,
    April has left me but lingering May.

"What tho' bright Summer is crownéd with roses?
    Deep in the forest arbutus doth hide;
I am the herald of all the rejoicing,
    Why must June always disown me?" she cried.

Down in the meadow she stoops to the daisies,
    Plucks the first bloom from the apple tree's
        bough,—
"Autumn will rob me of all the sweet apples,
    I will take one from her store of them now."

Summer is coming ! I hear the glad echo,
  Clearly it rings o'er the mountain and plain,
Sorrowful Spring leaves the beautiful woodlands,—
  Bright, happy Summer begins her sweet reign.

STRAWBERRIES.

WHEN the fields are sweet with clover,
    And the woods are glad with song,
When the brooks are running over,
    And the days are bright and long,
Then, from every nook and bower,
Peeps the dainty strawberry flower.

When the dear, enchanting Summer
    Tosses beauties at our feet,
She delights each weary comer
    With her berries, fresh and sweet :
Springtide's blossoms, stored away,
Ripen for us all to-day.

QUEEN HAREBELL.

DOWN in the meadow so tenderly green,
    Right in the heart of the mossiest dell,
Reigneth a queen, a bright happy queen,
        So graceful and tall
        At her feet we do fall,
For we know her and love her full well.

Or when the frail dew drops have melted away,
    And the sunlight is brighter and clearer,
Her heart doth rejoice in the beautiful day,
        Her eyes are so blue,
        So deep and so true,
Enchanted, we long to be near her.

And all the day long, in her rest and her peace,
    The birdies are singing her praises,
And when evening falls, and their happy songs cease
        She sinks to repose
        With the kingcup and rose,
Or is nodded good night by the daisies.

I love the fair lilies and roses so gay,
    They are rich in their pride and their splendor,
But still more do I love to wander away
          To the meadow so sweet,
          Where down at my feet,
The harebell blooms, modest and tender.

SUMMER.

HEAVEN'S glorious blue,
So deep, so pure, so fair !
And Summer's sunny air
Sweet with a fragrance rare
From flowers beyond compare,—
And all for you !

O happy, tender days !
O shades in forests deep,
And sweet, unbroken sleep,
And golden grain to reap,
And birds that always keep
Chanting their lays !

TRUE LOVE.

WHEN all the earth is fresh and green,
       And Heaven's azure smiling too,
When sunlight comes with golden gleam
And shimmers in the shallow stream,
   We say we know that Earth is sweet,
      And all the shining heavens true.

But when the clouds of wintry grey
       But dim the brightness of the sky,
And all our sunshine fades away,
Both out of doors and in, we say
   We know that Earth's few joys are fleet,
      And soon her fairest pleasures die.

So Friendship in her summer's hour
       Seems pure and clear as Heaven's blue,
But when the skies of Fortune lower,
With cruel frown they try her power,
   And find, tho' lovely for the time,
      She is, alas, how oft untrue !

O blest the love that does not go,
    But strengthens with each winter's blast !
That smiles when Fortune's light is low,
And smiles again to see it glow,
    That smiles in youth, in age, in prime,—
    Such love as this will always last.

SUNSHINE AND SHADOW.

SUNSHINE plays on the hillside steep,
  Or kisses the daisied meadow,
Leaving the forest and waters deep
    To quiet shadow.

When we pass thro' this life, this life below,
  When we find no flowery meadow,
Shall we wait and wait for the sun's bright glow,
    Or rest in shadow?

MEMORY.

THE years roll on, roll on, roll on,
　　The time flies swiftly by ;
We learn the more the more we grow,
At first we think, at last we know
　　How dear is memory !

And when our cares oppress our hearts,
　　As time flies swiftly by,
We smile, e'en thro' a mist of tears,
As we gaze back on happy years,
　　Thankful for memory.

And when we old and older grow,
　　And time has fast flown by,
Forgetting present joy or pain,
We live our childhood o'er again,—
　　Again in memory.

FROM SPRING TO FALL.

N field and forest, when 'twas bright
    With singing birds and starting flowers,
Sweet Springtime reigned ; her heart was light,
    She kissed the sunbeams, blest the showers,
She smiled upon the wayward breeze,
And clothed in tender green her trees.

Her banks were carpeted with grass,
    And purple with the violet ;
Her fresh leaves had a silken gloss,
    Her apple-blooms with dew were wet,
And fragrant, rosy buds did burst
Of sweet arbutus, opening first.

Then Summer took her flowery throne,
    With roses red and harebells blue,
With daisies in a moment blown,
    And feathery sprays of meadow rue,
With buttercups of shining gold,
And wealth of fairest flowers untold.

Her brooks ran babbling thro' her fields,
    Her snowy clouds went floating by,
Her happy birds their glad songs trilled,
    And soft and clear her azure sky,
Until, at last, her reign was o'er,
And Summer flowers bloomed no more.

Now Autumn, bright and fair, hath come,
    We welcome her with happy cry,—
About her head the gentians bloom,
    And at her feet her harvests lie ;
Her golden sheaves and stacks of grain
Show Summer's sun and Springtime's rain.

Her forests all are glowing bright,—
    Still withered leaves must soon drop down,
And when at last the ground is white,
    Sweet, shining Autumn drops her crown,
And Winter, with his icy breath,
Puts every bud and bloom to death.

THE SPIRIT OF THE FLOWERS.

OUT in the woods so tender,
  When the trees are green and fair,
Out in the shady forest,
  I can see her standing there ;
  Wrapt in her sunny hair,
  Out in the open air,
Out in the silent forest,
  I can see her standing there.

Long are the days, and pleasant,
  And the skies are bright and fair, —
Out in the sunny meadow,
  I can see her smiling there ;
  While the haystacks scent the air,
  And the flowers are fresh and rare,
Out in the blooming meadow,
  I can see her smiling there.

Down by the foamy brookside,
  Far from the sun's bright glare,
Mirrored against the waters,
  I can see her standing there ;

With the brier roses fair
Twined in her golden hair,—
Mirrored against the waters,
I can see her standing there.

After the day has faded,
Out in the chilly air,
Bathed in the dying purple,
I can see her standing there ;
Lovely beyond compare,
Free from all toil and care,—
Bathed in the dying purple
I can see her standing there.

Under the blue, blue heavens,
Under the stars so fair,
Out in the silver moonlight,
I can see her standing there ;
And the moonbeams, full and rare
They are woven in her hair,—
Out in the shining starlight,
I can see her smiling there.

Under the weeping willow,
With the brown leaves on her hair,
Out in the fading autumn,
I can see her weeping there,—

Frosty the autumn air,
Withered the flowers fair,—
Out in the dying autumn,
I can see her weeping there.

WHAT IS LEFT?

THE trees are barren, cold and brown,
   The snow is white on vale and hill,
The gentian, aster too, are gone,
   Is there no blossom with us still?

O look upon the hazel bough!
   The flowers there are bright as gold,
Tho' all is cold and wintry now,
   Their little petals still unfold.

The apples red have fallen down,
   And silent is the joyous rill,
The robin and the thrush have flown,
   Is there no bird to glad us still?

Hark! don't you hear a gladsome song,
   A merry chirp from tiny throat?—
The snowbird all the winter long
   Will cheer us with his happy note.

THE MONTHS.

JANUARY, icy cold,
   Leaves a mantle soft and white ;
February, sharp and bold,
   Onward takes his busy flight.

March's chilly breezes blow,
   Still they're touched by Winter's hand ;
April melts the frozen snow,
   April sunshine floods the land.

May awakes the sleeping flowers,
   Reigns a sweet and happy queen,
With her coaxing sun and showers
   Robes the trees in tender green.

June is bright with roses gay,
   Harebells bloom around her feet ;
Hot July rakes new-mown hay
   From the meadows, fresh and sweet.

August's pleasant, quiet reign
　Bids the meadow lilies come,
And September's golden grain
　Makes a welcome harvest-home.

Glad October's shining sun
　Paints the leaves in richest dyes,
And November, dreary one,
　Shoots his arrows as he flies.

Cold December's latest breath
　Makes the woods and meadows drear,
And his eyelids close in death
　As he ends the happy year.

'RAH FER TILDING!

ON a threshold, modest, lowly,
  In a humble cottage door,
Stood an old man, bent and hoary,
  Gazing, as we rode before;
Glasses on his time-worn eyes,
In his face a mild surprise,—
Shouting from his lonely building—
"'Rah fer Tilding! 'Rah fer Tilding!"

Rusty coat and battered breeches—
  Knowing no "*Intimidation!*"
Innocent of "*Fraud!*" "GREAT CRISIS!"
  Or "EXCITEMENT OF A NATION!"
Sweet and simple was his creed,
Noble heart was his indeed,
Free from vain or shallow gilding—
All his cry was "'Rah fer Tilding!"

THE GRUMBLER.

HIS YOUTH.

HIS cap was too thick, and his coat was too
thin ;
He couldn't be quiet ; he hated a din ;
He hated to write, and he hated to read ;
He was certainly very much injured indeed !
He must study and toil over work he detested ;
His parents were strict and he never was rested ;
He knew he was wretched as wretched could be,
There was no one so wretchedly wretched as he !

HIS MATURITY.

His farm was too small, and his taxes too big :
He was selfish, and lazy, and cross as a pig ;
His wife was too silly, his children too rude,
And just because he was uncommonly good !
He hadn't got money enough and to spare ;
He had nothing at all fit to eat or to wear !
He knew he was wretched as wretched could be,
There was no one so wretchedly wretched as he !

HIS OLD AGE.

He finds he has sorrows more deep than his fears,
He grumbles to think he has grumbled for years ;
He grumbles to think he has grumbled away
His home and his children, his life's little day :
But alas ! 'tis too late ! it is no use to say
That his eyes are too dim, and his hair is too grey ;
He knows he is wretched as wretched can be,
There *is* no one so wretchedly wretched as he !

A WINTER'S NIGHT.

THE sky is stormy grey, and frowns
    Upon the sunset's fading light ;
The angry wind still angrier sounds,
    And whistles to the Winter's night.

The snow is drifting thro' the air,
    To heap the plain with powdery white ;
The storm is fierce, the trees are bare,
    And dark and wild the Winter's night.

The moon amid the rifted cloud
    Is fain to hide her failing light ;
The sleet is sharp, the blast is loud,
    And bitter is the Winter's night.

A SUMMER'S NIGHT.

THE azure sky is rich and deep,
 With fleecy clouds of snowy white ;
The breezes sing you into sleep
 So gently on a Summer's night.

The whippoorwill, with plaintive cry,
 Rests from his eager, busy flight ;
The dewdrops on the grasses lie
 And sparkle thro' the Summer's night.

The moonbeams catch the first fair flush
 Of budding June with beauties bright ;
The creamy, half-blown roses blush,
 Unfolding thro' the Summer's night.

THE HUMMING-BIRD'S NEST.

WHEN June was bright with roses fair,
   And leafy trees about her stood,
When summer sunshine filled the air
   And flickered thro' the quiet wood,
There, in its shade and silent rest,
A tiny pair had built their nest.

And when July, with scorching heat,
   Had dried the meadow grass to hay,
And piled in stacks about the field,
   Or fragrant in the barn it lay,
Within the nest, so softly made,
Two tiny, snowy eggs were laid.

But when October's ripened fruit
   Had bent the very tree-tops down,
And dainty flowers faded, drooped,
   And stately forests lost their crown,
Their brood was hatched, and reared, and flown,—
The mossy nest was left alone.

And now the hills are cold and white,
   'Tis severed from its native bough ;
We gaze upon it with delight,—
   Where are its cunning builders now?
Far in the sunny South they roam,
And leave to us their Northern home.

WINTER.

SWEET autumn is no longer bright,
  And snow has wrapt the fields in white ;
    The little babbling rill,
That when the summer days were long,
Did cheer Sky Farm with merry song,
    Is icy, hushed and still.

Upon the meadow's rounded side,
The dainty flowers have drooped and died ;
    Those messengers of song,
That when the summer days were bright,
Have cheered Sky Farm with music light,
    To warmer climes have gone.

The icicles now fringe the trees
That swayed in summer's gentle breeze,
    When summer days were fair ;
That spread their branches far and high
Against her sunny, azure sky,—
    Now they are brown and bare.

Now sunlight glimmers, pale and shy,
And now the winter winds are high,
    The winter winds are bold :
We loved the springtime's sun and rain,
We longed for summer's rose again,
We loved the autumn's golden grain,—
    We love the winter's cold !

TEACH US HOW TO PRAY.

LORD, when we are led astray
    From the straight and narrow way,
Change our darkness into day,—
    Teach us how to pray.

When our path is dark and drear,
When our hearts are full of fear,
When our cross is hard to bear,
    Teach us how to pray.

MARCH.

THE swollen brook, the muddy stream,
   The sun's uncertain, quivering gleam,
The bare brown earth, and skies that seem
To smile and frown on every dream
         Of Spring, for which we search:

The soft, warm, dreamy springtime air,
The tiny plants so green and fair,
The budding willow catkins, where
The breezes Spring's first fragrance bear,
         All tell us it is March.

The springtime rains that gently fall,
And water, wake, and freshen all,
The starting trees, so straight and tall,
The robin's note, the bluebird's call,—
         First songs that say so much!

The consciousness that Spring is here,—
Sweet Spring, to every heart so dear!
The newness of the opening year,
The mingled joy, and hope, and fear,
         All tell us it is March.

WHO STARTS THE FLOWERS?

HAPPY Sunshine smiled one day,
    Raindrops chased her light away,--
" Don't you see the grass is brown ?
We must patter, patter down,
Till the earth has had its fill."
Sunshine answered, smiling still :—
" Don't you see the ground is bare ?
Flowers should be starting there,
But they will not come for rain,
I must make them bloom again."

Then the Breeze came hurrying past
With a fresh, life-giving blast :—
" It is I, too, help to make
All the lovely flowers wake ;
Blowing thro' the sleeping trees
What will rouse them like the breeze ?"

Said the Night :—"I, as I creep,
Close their leaves and bring them sleep ;
With the cloak that darkest seems,
Shut their eyes to pleasant dreams."

Said the Day :—" I, with my light,
Change the gloomy robe of Night
To the shining one of Day,
Driving all its shades away."

Said the Earth :—" I feed the flowers,
Lavish on them all my powers ;
Close entrusted to my care,
Planted in my bosom fair,
When their dainty buds appear,
I, their mother, hold them dear."

Said the Sky :—" I bend above,
Tenderly to watch and love.
'Neath my azure arch they live ;
Sun and rain are mine to give."

Cried the Spring, who heard them all :—
" Sunbeams, shine ! and showers, fall !
I have broken Winter's spell,
You must rear my darlings well ;
By my magic breath they start,
Let them cheer each drooping heart ! "

FAIRY LAND.

FAIRY LAND is far away,—
    Over mountains capped with snow,
Over seas of silver spray,
    In the sunset's parting glow :
There flowers are blooming all the year,
And skies are always bright and clear,—
O, never there 'tis bleak or drear,
    In happy Fairy Land !

Fairy Land is far away,
    Yet 'tis ever just in sight,—
Haunting all our weary way
    With its visions of delight :
There care or sorrow never seems
To weigh our hearts, or blight our dreams ;
And every pleasure brighter beams
    In happy Fairy Land.

Fairy Land is far away !
    We may look, and long, and wait,
We may hasten, or delay,
    But we always come too late ;

Tho' rich with promise bloom its flowers,
Its witching fruits are never ours :
Farewell, O sweet, delusive bowers
    Of happy Fairy Land !

MAY.

WAFTED thro' the silent woodland
    Comes a breath of brighter days,
And the distant hills are shrouded
  In a dreamy, purple haze ;
O what joy to see the flowers,
  Hidden 'neath the snow so long,
And to hear the silence broken
  By a sudden burst of song !

Now the tender, sweet arbutus
  Trails her blossom-clustered vines,
And the many-fingered cinquefoil
  In the shady hollow twines ;
Here, behind this crumbled tree-trunk,
  With the cooling showers wet,
Fresh and upright, blooms the sunny
  Golden-yellow violet.

Now the phœbe and the robin
  Bid farewell to winter's cold,
And in yonder marshes burns
  The fiery-flaming marigold ;

Or where alders fringe the water,
  Casting perfume on the air,
See the purple trilliums blooming
  Rich and stately, everywhere.

O how sweet, how sweet is springtime !
  When the meadow dons her green,
And the tangled woods are fairest,
  And the sunlight shifts between ;
Fresh and pure her crown of blossoms,
  Thick with flowers all her way,
While the blue skies bent above her,
  Deep and tender, smile on May.

A BIT OF WOODS.

LITTLE gushing brook o'erhung by trees,
  The stately chestnut and wide-spreading oak ;
The wind that whispers low, as if it spoke
To birds and blossoms there,—a quiv'ring breeze ;
A shadow on the ground, where you can trace
  The graceful outlines of the trees above,
That stir whenever breezes shake the boughs,
  And silently and softly bend and move.

The purple blossoms that are flung around ;
  The faint anemones that trembling blush ;
  The carol of the bluebird or the thrush,
And fair arbutus trailing on the ground ;
The sun that smiles upon them from the sky,
  And throws his rays between the tree-tops tall ;
The bee that buzzes in the flower cups ;
  The sense of peaceful stillness over all.

TO THE SWALLOWS.

DEAR birds, that greet us with the spring,
   That fly along the sunny blue,
That hover 'round your last year's nests,
   Or cut the shining heavens through ;
That skim along the meadow grass
   Among the flowers sweet and fair ;
That croon upon the pointed roof,
   Or, quiv'ring, balance in the air ;
Ye heralds of the summer days,
   As quick you dart across the lea,
Though other birds be fairer, yet
   The dearest of them all are ye.

Dear as the messengers of Spring,
   Before the buds have opened wide,
Dear when the other birds are here,
   ˙ Dear in the burning summertide ;

But when the lonely autumn wind
  About the flying forest grieves,
In vain we look for you, and find
  Your empty nests beneath the eaves !

SPRING SCATTERS FAR AND WIDE.

ON every bank, in every nook,
  By every shaded, sparkling brook,
    On every mountain side,
In every hollow, deep and cool,
By every wood-road, every pool,
    Wherever sunbeams glide ;
In every shadow, long and deep,
Where all the heavens seem asleep,—
    Wherever mosses hide,
In rich luxuriance, everywhere,
Her flowers, delicate and fair,
    Spring scatters far and wide.

Upon the mossy apple bough
The rosy blooms are trembling now,
And in the woods a fragrance rare
Of wild azaleas fills the air,
And richly tangled overhead
We see their blossoms sweet and red ;
The strawbell and the columbine
Their buff and crimson flowers entwine,

And thick in many a sunny spot
There blooms the pale forget-me-not ;
The modest, lowly violet
In leaves of tender green is set,
So rich she cannot hide from view,
But covers all the bank with blue.
Her birds and bees so glad and gay,
Her songs, as rich and full to-day
   As in the summertide,
Her beauties, dewy fresh and sweet,
Her blossoms, cluster'd round our feet,
   Spring scatters far and wide.

IT SEEMS AS IF THE FLOWERS WERE ALIVE.

IT seems as if the flowers were alive,—
   They bend and bow to one another so,
As if they had a secret that they told
By opening their eyes of blue and gold,
   And looking, and by nodding to and fro.

It seems as if the flowers were alive,—
   And all unlike in color, form, and size,
They bear a family resemblance, yet
There *is* a secret, which we cannot get,
   That in their rosy-blushing petals lies.

It seems as if the flowers were alive,—
   As grouped together in the fields they stand,
As if to nearer press, that every vine
About them might its tendril fingers twine,—
   Looking like fairy sisters hand in hand.

It seems as if the flowers were alive,—
　Some love the sunlight, others love the shade ;
Some climb the cold rocks on the mountain
　　height,
And others make the dusty roadsides bright ;
　Some love the brook and some the mellow
　　glade.

It seems as if the flowers were alive,—
　Warm, rich and passionate, or sweet and shy,
Or pure and spotless, throwing on the air
Their fragrance, budding, blooming, fresh and fair,
　At last they slowly wither, fade and die.

A SUMMER SHOWER.

MIST upon the mountain top
    Slowly settles down,
Rain is gathering, drop by drop,
    Skies begin to frown ;
In the field and in the lane,
    Many a downcast flower
Droopeth, longing for the rain,
    For the summer shower.

Now the rain begins to fall
    From its cloudy bed,—
Listen ! hear the thrushes call !
    Clover lifts her head,—
Shrunken streamlets rise and swell ;
    From each leafy bough
Jewels hang, and in the dell
    Grasses bend and bow.

Mist upon the mountain top
    Lightly sails away ;
Rain has fallen, drop by drop,
    Blue replaces grey ;

In the field and in the lane,
Many a freshened flower
Smileth, brightened by the rain,
By the summer shower.

THE BOBOLINK'S NEST.

WHERE the flowers are fresh and fragrant
    Where the noonday shadows fall,
Where the warm, delicious sunlight
        Smiles so true ;
Where the breezes leave their ripples,
   Blowing thro' the grasses tall,
Daisies whiten all the meadows,
        Skies are blue.

There, when apple-blooms had fallen,
   Rosy petals strewn the ground,
Springtime melted into Summer,
        All was rest ;
And a merry, white-capped darling,
   With his mate so quaint and brown,
Underneath the tufted grasses
        Built their nest.

Softly lined and loosely woven,
   Light blue eggs were in it laid,
Clear, transparent, blotched with purple,
        Fair to see ;

While the mother covered closely,
　　Anxious, tender, half afraid,
Bob o'Lincoln carolled to her
　　　　Full of glee.

But one day as she was brooding,
　　With four eggs beneath her breast,
Came a sudden rush upon her,—
　　　　Up she flew !
All her dainty eggs were broken,
　　And they took the empty nest ;—
What to her tho' flowers are fragrant,
　　　　Skies are blue !

HAYMAKING.

DAISIED meadows, fields of clover,
  Grasses juicy, fresh and sweet,—
In a day the wild bees hover
  Over many a fragrant heap ;
Windrows all the meads do cover,
  Blossoms fall, and farmers reap,—
In a month, and all is over—
  Stored away for winter's keep.

A MIDSUMMER DAY.

O WHAT is so sweet as a midsummer day,
    When no sound greets the ear save a bird's
      happy lay,
Or the rustling of leaves as the wind passes thro';
When the earth is so green, and the sky is so blue!

When the swallows in ecstasy dart thro' the air,
When the breeze is so pure, and the flowers are so
    fair,
When the grain is so golden, the farmer so gay,
O what can compare with a midsummer day!

OUR CHICKENS.

GENTLE pullet on the stoop,—
   A rooster where the cream is rising,—
A hen who doubtless likes our soup,
   And eats it without criticizing !

A mild-eyed chicken calmly stands
   And on the kitchen table lingers,—
And why ? Of course he understands
   The bread is fresh from mamma's fingers.

An angry "shoo ! "—he thinks it vain,
   But then of course there is no knowing,—
He smashes thro' a window pane
   And fears it's time that he was going.

A pullet, *not* upon the stoop,
   But with cream gravy on a platter ;
A hen who's grown so fat on soup
   That what she *makes* is no small matter.

Ah, chickens! 'tis no use to beg,
    Tho' you were bold, we, we are bolder,—
And mamma, will you take a leg?
    Or would you rather have a shoulder?

You make a most delicious pie!
    Your time is past and ours beginning,—
Not long upon my plate you'll lie,—
    This is the penalty of sinning!

IN THE LOFT.

IN the hay-loft, dark and sweet,
    With the breath of new-mown hay ;
There the lights and shadows fall
Weird upon the seamed, scarred wall,
And the dusky swallows soar
High above the broken floor,
Lightly poise on tiny feet,
    Quiver, dip, and dart away.

HIGH AND LOW.

THE showers fall as softly
   Upon the lowly grass,
As on the stately roses
   That tremble as they pass.

The sunlight shines as brightly
   On fern leaves bent and torn,
As on the golden harvest,—
   The fields of waving corn.

The wild birds sing as sweetly
   To rugged, jagged pines,
As to the shaded orchards
   And to the cultured vines.

Our Father looks as kindly
   Upon the lowly poor,
As on the rich and haughty
   Who turn them from their door.

AFTER THE RAIN.

GRASS is newly fresh and green,
        After the rain ;
Sky is fair in brighter sheen,
        After the rain ;
Out upon the mountain side
Floating shadows softly glide,
        After the rain.

Flowers are fresh and leaves are bright,
        After the rain ;
Sunshine floods the land with light,
        After the rain ;
Morning vapors melt away,
Birds are singing glad and gay,
        After the rain.

All the earth seems pure and clear,
        After the rain ;
Gloomy troubles disappear
        After the rain ;
Sunshine comes with sudden glow,
Hearts are glad, and sorrows go,
        After the rain.

AT DAWN.

GLIMMERING of greyish light,
  Before the morning breaks ;
The weary death of weary night,
  Before the daytime wakes ;
And rosy tints in melting skies,
As morning opes her dewy eyes.

A sudden gleam, a deepening glow,
  Behind the sun-lined cloud ;
While fresh and clear the breezes blow,
  And birds are calling loud,
And long, dark shadows lowly lie
Where stately trees are standing high.

And so, with first uncertain gleams,
  Before the brighter hours,
We see suggested hopes and dreams
  That still shall show their flowers ;
Till, as the quickened morning wakes,
A fuller light upon us breaks.

SIGHTS AND SOUNDS OF SUMMER.

SILVER rains falling on blossoms and leaves;
 Song of the brook in the valley below;
Harvdest fields stacked with the lightly bound
  sheaves;
Twitter of swallows in under the eaves,
 Waking to life at the morning's first glow.

Sun looking down on the newly mown hay;
 Chirp of the cricket, and hum of the bee;
Happy birds singing and winging their way;
Flowers in the meadow, so rosy and gay;
 Cool, gentle breezes that pass o'er the lea.

Bright daylight fading adown in the west,
 Silver moon rising, so glowing and bright;
Little birds sleeping 'neath mother's warm breast;
All the earth hushed in the stillness of rest,
 Lighted by fireflies that gleam thro' the night.

SLEEP.

WHEN the evening shadows creep
      Stealthily,
Hiding every hill and dale,
Hiding all things with their veil ;
  When the shining day doth die,
    Sweet is sleep.

When the evening shadows creep
      Stealthily ;
To the baby in her nest,
Longing for her quiet rest,
  Hushed by loving lullaby,
    Sweet is sleep.

When the evening shadows creep
      Stealthily,
To the weary heart and brain
Bringing tranquil peace again ;
  All our cares and sorrows fly,—
    Sweet is sleep.

AN AUTUMN PICTURE.

SKY deep, intense, and wondrous blue,
   With clouds that sail the heavens thro';
And mountain slopes so broad and fair,
With here and there amongst the green,
A maple or an ash tree seen
   In glowing color, bright and rare.

Green fields, where silvery ripples fade,
With cattle resting in the shade;
   Far mountains touched with purple haze,
That, like a veil of morning mist,
By gleams of golden sunlight kissed,
   Seems but a breath of bygone days.

And clover, which has bloomed anew
Since shining scythes did cut it thro';
   And corn fields with their harvest fair;
And golden rod upon the hill,
And purple asters blooming still, —
   And sunlight melted into air.

ONE MOMENT MORE.

IN Spring a new life stirs the air,
    It falls in soft, refreshing showers,
'Tis melted into sunbeams clear,
    The sunbeams wake the sleeping flowers,—
O then we cry,—"Thou changeful Spring,
One moment more, sweet Spring, delay !"—
But Spring has come, and passed away.

In Summer all the earth is fair,
    And rich and bright her flowers bloom,
Her glad birds sing in meadows wide,
    And in the forest's shaded gloom,
And then we cry,—"O linger still !
A little longer, Summer, stay !"—
But Summer came, and passed away.

O Autumn ! with your harvest stores,
    Your golden grain, your merry cheer,
Your long, full days of sunlight warm,
    You bear the fruit of all the year,—
Then bring to us your ripened nuts,
And bring to us your asters gay !—
Ere long you too shall pass away.

INDIAN SUMMER.

WEARY, weary are the days
    When Fall has ceased to reign,
When Winter cold, and bleak, and drear,
    Has scarcely chilled his clouds to grey,
    Has scarcely killed the flowers gay,
Before he ends the dying year,—
    Then weary are the days.

But, from October's rustling leaves,
    October's golden grain,—
From shining forests, rich, aglow,
    And flying birds, and sun that warms,
    He cannot change her smiles to storms,
He cannot change the grass to snow
At once, from fair October's glow.

And so, between them comes a pause
    In grey November's chill,
A sweet, and soft, and languid breath ;

Until our thoughts we reconcile
To Winter's frown from Summer's smile,
And learn to bear the Autumn's death,
Ere Winter breaks the pause.

THROUGH THE BRANCHES.

IN Summer, thro' the leafy trees
  That spread their branches high,
I catch between the quivering leaves,
  A scrap of shining sky ;
The sunlight flickers on the grass.
  It dances here and there,—
The soft wind breathes of forest glades
  And meadows broad and fair.

And when October's gentians deep
  Are standing bright and blue,
I see a softer, hazier sky,
  The glowing branches thro' ;
I see a snowy, sailing cloud,
  The rosy leaves between,
I see the golden mountain top
  With pine trees darkly green.

But in November, I can see
  Thro' branches spreading bare,
A cold and grey November sky
  That once had looked so fair ;

Behind the branches I can see
   The snowflakes floating white,
The mountain top so lone and brown,
   The sunset's waning light.

AUTUMN'S DYING.

HERE and there, thro' the frosty air,
 The withered leaves are blowing,
The forests stand all stiff and bare,
 For Autumn's going, going.

The birds have ceased their carols gay,
 The brooks their joyous flowing,
The heavy clouds are wintry grey,
 For Autumn's going, going.

A month ago, the woods were bright
 With colors rich and glowing,
But the last leaf will fall to-night,—
 For Autumn's going, going.

The ground is white with Winter's snow,
 The flakes are whirling, flying,
The whistling winds still sharper blow,
 For Autumn's dying, dying.

The clouds are gathering thick and fast,
    And on the mountains lying,
The sharp wind blows a bitter blast,
    To mourn the Autumn's dying.

TO A DEAD LEAF.

 WITHERED leaf ! O sailing leaf !
    That flutters here and there,
With you the spirit of the Fall
    Is flying far away ;
You speak of dreary Autumn's death,
  Of Winter bleak and bare ;
You speak of angry wind and snow,
    And skies of gloomy grey.

O withered leaf ! O sailing leaf !
  Wrapt in your crumpled brown,
You know the tenderness of Spring,
    The Summer's rich array ;
You caught the glory of the Fall
  Before you fluttered down ;
You hold the glow and heat and light
    In which you past away.

O withered leaf ! O sailing leaf !
  When buried 'neath the snow,
When buried 'neath the cruel snow
    That holds you captive long,

Shall you remember all the joys
   That came so long ago?
And from the distance shall you catch
   The echo of my song?

BLOW.

BLOW, blow, thou bitter wind,
  And heap the scattered leaves !
Blow, blow, thou changeful wind,
  And heap the drifting snow !
Ripple the noonday grass,
  Or rustle 'mongst the sheaves,
Or wake the tender Spring,—
      Blow, blow !

Blow, blow, thou Summer wind
  In whispers far away !
Blow, blow, thou sighing wind
  In murmurs faint and low !
Thro' woodlands quick with song,
  And meadows sweet with hay,
O perfume-laden wind,
      Blow, blow !

Blow, blow, thou Winter wind,
  And beat the frosty air !
Blow, blow, thou angry wind,
  The year is lying low !

Pile up the scurrying clouds,
   And make the new year fair ;
O wild and wailing wind,
     Blow, blow !

LET US THANK OUR FATHER DEAR.

FOR mellow pears we have gathered in,
  For rosy apples, and well-filled bin,
    That tell of a fruitful year ;
For golden grain that is stored away,
For fragrant piles of the clover hay,
    Let us thank our Father dear.

For a new-found joy, or a new-made friend,
For sweet, fair flowers to love and tend;
    For the merry winter cheer ;
For the snowflakes white, and the voices gay,
For our happy and sweet, and loving day,
    Let us thank our Father dear.

For the year that is past and the year to come,
For the ripened stores of our harvest home,
    For the home that blossoms here ;
For the thoughts and fancies that 'round it cling
For the hearts that love, and the lips that sing,
    Let us thank our Father dear.

SNOWDRIFTS.

HOW cold the snow, how pure and white !
  How deep the shadows on it lie !
 Above them bends a soft blue sky
With streaming sunshine warm and bright.

The snow was swirled by angry blast
  And sent adrift thro' frosty air,
  But now it lies in silence there,
With all its troubled tumult past.

In dazzling splendor, dazzling white,
  Rounded and curved, how pure the snow !
  How clear and cold the world below !
The world above how calm and bright !

THE SNOWBIRD.

WHEN the leaves are shed,
And the branches bare,
When the snows are deep,
And the flowers asleep,
And the autumn dead ; ·
And the skies are o'er us bent,
Grey and gloomy, since she went,
And the sifting snow is drifting
Thro' the air ;

Then, 'mid snowdrifts white,
Though the trees are bare,
Comes the snowbird, bold
In the winter's cold ;
Quick and round, and bright,
Light he steps across the snow,
Cares he not for winds that blow,
Tho' the sifting snow be drifting
Thro' the air.

FRIENDSHIP.

STRONG as the ship that braves the blast
  Upon a stormy sea ;
Deep as the ocean's rippling tides,
  So shall our friendship be.

Firm as the anchor, buried far
  Beneath a rolling sea ;
Pure as the sky above it bent,
  So shall our friendship be.

SPRING IS HERE.

WIND, be still, 'tis Spring!
   Sun, shine bright and clear!
Birds, fly northward—sing!
   Spring is here!

Snowdrifts, melt, 'tis Spring!
   Make her pathway clear,
Make the forest ring,
   Spring is here!

May shall bring us flowers,
   April, smile and tear,
March prepares the hours—
   March is here!

FLOWN AWAY.

ON the bare, brown boughs before me,
   In the softly falling rain,
Rests a bluebird,—now, upstarting,
See how suddenly she's darting
   Far away across the plain.

It was but a dash of color
   Shown against a stormy sky,
Only two blue wings uplifted
When the grey clouds slowly drifted,—
   But they bore a song on high.

She is lost in misty darkness,—
   Will she pierce beyond the grey?
Will she reach the blue behind it?
Will she pause when she shall find it?
   Will she know it? Who can say!

WHEN shall Springtime cheer us,
　　When, ah when ?
When fair June is near us,
　　Then, ah then !
Then the trees shall burst in leaf,
Winter shall forget his grief ;
Winds shall all forget to moan
In their wild and wintry tone ;
Gentle breezes then shall play
Thro' the fragrant woods of May,
Birds shall seek a Northern home,
Bees and flowers together come :
When shall Springtime cheer us,
　　When, ah when ?
When fair June is near us,
　　Not till then !

AN APRIL RAIN.

THE drops are falling, falling
    Upon the window-pane,
The birds are calling, calling
    Thro' wood, and vale, and plain,—
    It is an April rain.

O, see the clear drops glisten
    In many a pearly chain !
O, hear the phœbe—listen !
    O, hear the plaintive strain
    Sung thro' the April rain.

The clear, fresh wind is blowing,
    The grass grows green again,
The brook is overflowing,
    And sings a glad refrain
    Thro' whispering April rain.

The drops are falling, falling
    Upon the window-pane,
The birds are calling, calling
    Thro' wood, and hill, and plain,—
    It is an April rain.

APRIL! APRIL! ARE YOU HERE?

APRIL! April! are you here?
    O how fresh the wind is blowing!
See! the sky is bright and clear,
    O how green the grass is growing!
            April! April!
                Are you here?

April! April! is it you?
    See how fair the flowers are springing!
Sun is warm and brooks are clear,
    O how glad the birds are singing!
            April! April!
                Is it you?

April! April! you are here!
    Tho' your smiling turn to weeping,
Tho' your skies grow cold and drear,
    Tho' your gentle winds are sleeping,
            April! April!
                You are here!

A WELCOME.

WELCOME to the winds of Spring,
   Welcome to the starting flowers,
Welcome to the birds that sing,
   Welcome to the springtide hours !
Tho' the winds be wild and high,
   There's a newness in them blown,
That the Summer's languid sigh,
   Distant murmur, does not own.
There's a warmness in the sun,
   There's a fragrance in the air,
There's a blueness in the sky
   Winter skies may never wear.
There's a greenness in the field
   Where the babbling brooklets flow,
There's a freshness in the songs
   Later birds may never know.
Welcome, then, to winds of Spring !
   Welcome to the starting flowers,
Welcome to the birds that sing,
   Welcome to the springtide hours !

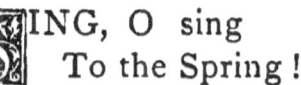ING, O sing
         To the Spring!
What did April bring?
She brought us violets blue and shy,
   She brought us windflowers white and frail,
She brought a warm and tender sky,
   And life in every gale.
         Sing, O sing
         To the Spring!
   These, and more, did April bring.

IN THE WOODS.

FAR away in shadowy woodlands,
   Where a footstep never falls,—
There the Spring is late and shy,
There the pink arbutus opens,
   And the plaintive phœbe calls,
There the living sunlight glances
Thro' a changeful April sky.

There, in new delight, the robin
   Chants alone his morning lay,
And the bluebird singing flies ;
There, 'mid leafy glooms, the thrushes
   Trill their fuller roundelay,
Or the echoes' quick vibrations
Answer to their restless cries.

There the rich and lavish Summer,
   With her roses, tangled bloom,
Comes and goes unheeded by ;
Blending in a dusky splendor,
   Light, and color, and perfume,

Dainty ferns and dewy mosses,
Flowers, and leaves, and deep blue sky.

Autumn comes in glowing colors,
   Stands a moment in a flame,—
Then she loses all her crown,
And her purple and her crimson,
   Burning, fade and fall again,
Flying thro' the dusky forest
In a whirl of crumpled brown.

Far away in shadowy woodlands,
   In the Spring the soft winds blow,
Murmuring to the rustling leaves ;—
But no voice shall break the silence,
   And no footprint crush the snow,
When the wilder blast of Winter
Thro' the empty forest grieves.

BEFORE A STORM.

WITH a close, heavy stillness
    The air is oppressed,
There is rain in the east,
    There are clouds in the west ;
Grey billows of vapor
    Roll silently on,
To shut out the sky
    And the warm, gracious sun.

AFTER A STORM.

WITH a freshness and sweetness
   The air is made new ;
The birds are all singing,
   The skies are all blue ;
The flowers have uplifted
   Their petals again,
And the meadows grow green
   At the touch of the rain.

SOFTLY, SOFTLY DIE AWAY.

SOFTLY, softly die away
 Glowing colors of the day,
Failing lights are pale and wan
When the setting sun is gone ;
And that red streak in the sky
Shows that even day must die.

Softly creeps the evening on
When the radiant day is gone,
One by one the stars gleam forth,
East and west, and south and north,
Softly chilly twilight goes,
Softly comes the night's repose.

IN THE SPRING.

HOW sweet the woods are in the Spring !
　　When no frosty chill of Winter lingers,
Murmuring breezes, as they come and go
　　Seem caressing you with loving fingers ;
And the sky is soft and hazy blue,
　　With the snowy clouds across it flying,
And the thrushes fill the air with song,
　　And the winds are whispering and sighing.

O how fresh the fields are in the Spring !
　　When the brooks are singing, dancing, leaping,
And the grass has lifted high its head,
　　And the wild flowers have awaked from sleeping;
With their ferns in patches dewy-sweet,
　　With their fragrant leaves and juicy clover,
Trees of misty green, so lately bare,
　　And the sweet spring sunlight falling over.

O how faint the hills are in the Spring !
　　When from clouds the eye has scarce defined
　　　them,

In their blueness but a dream of blue,
    With the sunset glowing red behind them ;
With a purple haze before them drawn,
    Like a curtain, indistinctly veiling,
And we feel the loveliness beyond,
    As the sunset lights are slowly failing.

O how happy homes are in the Spring !
    Maples round the door grow green and tender,
Sweet air comes thro' windows open thrown,
    Springtime conquers—Winter must surrender ;
Trills of happy bird-song from without
    Fill the air with music, clearer, sweeter ;
To the garden Spring has kissed her hand,
    And the flowers all rise up to greet her.

O how sweet our thoughts are in the Spring !
    Every heart is filled with true thanksgiving,
Steeped in sunlight and with music stirred
    In the dear delight of all things living ;
Happy memories of other Springs,
    Summer's roses ever drawing nearer,—
In our hearts all love reflected lies,
    As the green trees in the lake's broad mirror.

BIRTHDAY SONG—TO H. S. G.

(May 19th, 1878.)

ALL dappled with clouds is the warm blue
  sky,
 And steeped in sunlight the green earth lies,
The south wind murmurs drowsily by
 In fainting whispers and dreamy sighs ;
It brings its fancies from mountain and lea,
 It brings its fancies from far and near,
It catches a birthday song for me,
 And breathes it into my ear :—

  " Thro' many a forest have I flown,
   And many a hillside seen,
  And many a silvery furrow blown
   Thro' rippling fields of green ;
  But never did I know a hill
   So broad and fair as this,
  Nor such a pure and sparkling rill
   Has it been my lot to kiss."

" Full many a rustling tree I've bent,
   And opened many a flower ;
And each and all a greeting sent
   On this most happy hour.
The cold grey rocks, so hard and stern,
   A birthday greeting send,
For even a senseless stone will turn
   To thank a loving friend."

All dappled with clouds is the warm blue sky,
   And steeped in sunlight the green earth lies,
The south wind murmurs drowsily by
   In fainting whispers and dreamy sighs ;
How gladly and joyously ripple the rills
   On this brightest and best of the New Year's
   days,
How dimly outlined the distant hills
   In their fold of purple haze.

WHO BRINGS IN THE SUMMER?

WHEN we bid good-bye to Spring,
    Full of joys that June shall bring,
When we hear the glad birds sing
    " June, thou joyous comer !"
There's a sweetness in the air,
There's a languid fragrance there,
Maytide breezes did not bear,—
    Who brings in the Summer?

Babbling brook and fluttering breeze,
Sunset, golden thro' the trees,
Butterflies and humming bees,—
    June, the latest comer !
Sunlight, glancing in between
Chestnut leaves of olive green,—
Meadows, quiet and serene,
    These bring in the Summer.

Birds that happy songs repeat,
Apple-blossoms, rosy-sweet,
Scattered petals at our feet,
    June, the gladdest comer !

Clear blue sky, so deep and fair,
Trembling depths of azure air,
Wild azaleas, red and rare,
  These bring in the Summer.

Wild birds, sing your merriest strain,
Bid good-bye to springtime's reign,
Welcome in fair June again,
  June, the happiest comer !
Let our thoughts be light and gay,
Care and sorrow far away,
So with thankful hearts to-day
  We'll bring in the Summer.

MAIDEN'S HAIR.

WITH A GIFT OF PRESSED FERNS.

WHERE the tinkling water-falls
   Sparkle over rocky ledges,
Where the slate-grey catbird calls
   In and out the tangled hedges,
     Green and slender, spreading fair,
     You may see the maiden's hair.

'Tis as tho' some lady left
   By the stream her floating tresses
Long ago, and now, bereft,
   Where they be she little guesses,—
     But they still are tossing there,
     And we call them maiden's hair.

Then may these a picture bring
   Of green alders overhanging,
Of a wind-blown brook in Spring,
   And a thousand ripples, clanging
     In a silver mingling, where
     Nods the slender maiden's hair.

Tho' their grace more formal be
　Than when by the brook they fluttered,
Touched by winds that lazily
　In among the tree-tops muttered,
　　Still the same quaint charm they bear
　　Of the earliest maiden's hair.

SUNSET.

CHANGEFUL light, suffused in rosy
blushes,—
 The sunset sky has many a crimson stain,
Across the east the fainting splendor flushes,
And far beyond the western hills,
 In snatches, gleams again.

A soft grey sky with floating mists upon it,
 Warm purple-brown, and flecked and fringed
   with rose ;
The dark blue mountains stand as painted on it
In fading lights, and misty folds,
 And fast dissolving hues.

O sunset, deepening in your golden shadows !
 O sunset, widening in your rosier glow !
Your flush has fall'n as fair on daisied meadows
As when the winter skies have lent
 Their pinkness to the snow !

WHAT DO YOU SEE?

OVER the meadows cast your eye,—
     What do you see?
   O Life in its many phases!
From the birds that sing and the wings that soar,
And the bee that hums as he gathers his store,
   To the brooks and the trees and the daisies,—
     These you may see—and more.

Into the forest cast your eye,
     What do you see?
   O, Silence in all its phases!
From the rocks that stand as they long have stood,
And the shadows that fall across the wood,
   To the skies, and the distant hazes,—
     These you may see—and more.

Into your own heart cast your eye,—
     What do you see?
   O, Thought in its many phases!

From Right that struggles to conquer Wrong,
And Love that is pure and Friendship strong,
   To fancy's wildering mazes,—
      These you may see—and more.

A SKY of scurrying clouds
    That fly on dappled sails,
And with purple oars,
To the sunset shores
    Are blown by the evening gales.

They reach the golden gate,
    They catch the golden glow,
And, with purple oars,
At the sunset shores
    They wait, while the winds breathe low.

A LULLABY.

THE sun is behind the western hills,
  The purple fades, and the red lights die ;
The faint stars sleep when the day is bright,
But they watch for baby all the night,—
            Lullaby !

While day still lingers the robin sings,
  And echoes deep in the wood reply,
But when the earth is no longer light,
The whippoorwill sings to the darkling night,—
            Lullaby !

Over the mountain there comes a glow,
  The clouds break up in the eastern sky ;
The moon is shining so round and bright,
And walks the heavens thro' all the night,—
            Lullaby !

The deep green vine to the window creeps,
  By night winds stirred as they flutter by,

And with clasping tendrils, clinging tight,
It peeps at the baby the livelong night,—
                    Lullaby !

O stronger than moon and stars in one,—
    O pure and true as the midnight sky,—
Love is forever warm and bright,
Guarding the baby day and night,—
                    Lullaby !

RIPE GRAIN.

STILL, white face of perfect peace,
  Untouched by passion, freed from pain !
He, who ordained that work should cease,
  Took to Himself the ripened grain.

O noble face ! your beauty bears
  The glory that is wrung from pain,—
The high, celestial beauty wears
  Of finished work, of ripened grain.

Of human care you left no trace,
  No lightest trace of grief or pain,—
On earth an empty form and face—
  In Heaven stands the ripened grain.

PURPOSES.

UPON the broad, green mountain side
　　There are so many moss-grown nooks
Thro' ample meadows, flowering wide,
　　There flow so many singing brooks,
　　　　The purple asters o'er them lean,
　　　　The flickering shadows fall between,
　　　　The maples tremble, all day long,
　　　　With shifting wind or passing song.

And every leaf, on every tree,
　　Must start with Spring and fade with Fall,
And every brook must reach the sea,
　　And sunbeams quiver over all ;
　　　　And every bloom must be a bud,
　　　　And every oak-tree in the wood
　　　　Within an acorn-cup must lie,
　　　　And every bird must learn to fly.

And every cloud must fall to earth,
　　In silent shower, or stormy spray,
And every man, whate'er his birth,
　　Must learn, at last, to pass away ;

And every heart must learn to beat,
As every robin learns to trill,—
And every life be made complete,
Led upward by a higher Will.

NOTE.—Excepting the first poem of each author, these verses are arranged, virtually, in the order in which they were written, the earliest poems given, in each case, being written at the age of nine years. *Fairyland* and *'Rah fer Tilding* were written in common. *The Farm Beyond the Hills* has reference to an outlook between near ridges, upon distant mountains and vales.

www.ingramcontent.com/pod-product-compliance
Lightning Source LLC
Chambersburg PA
CBHW030132060726
47499CB00015B/1434